BOOKS BY C.K. SORENS

TRIMARKED SERIES

Trimarked
Afflicted
Tattered

***

THE DJINN OF LAS VEGAS

Eighteen Wishes

This novel contains content that may be triggering.
For a list of possible triggers, please visit
https://www.cksorens.com/trimarked-trigger-warnings

This is a work of fiction. All of the characters, organizations, and events portrayed in this novel are products of the author's imagination.

For those who fight to be heard,
and the ones who refuse to disappear.

C.K. SORENS

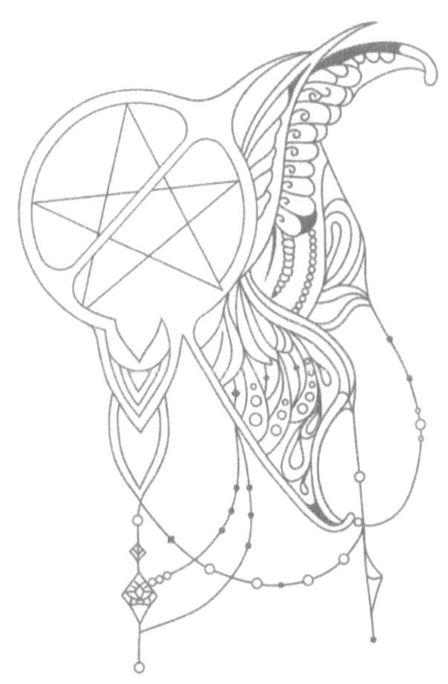

TATTERED

TRIMARKED SERIES
BOOK THREE

1

EMBER

The throwaways of Trifectan society crowded the Underground Club, clinging to the comfort of forgetting the dangers above. Stale air pressed down like a heavy blanket, laced with the faint tang of sweat, old alcohol, and the lingering scent of burnt wire. Dim lights flickered overhead, casting long, restless shadows across the worn concrete floors.

In the pre-dawn hush, older Halfers lay sprawled along mismatched armchairs and sagging couches, their uneven breathing the only sign that they hadn't faded away entirely. The furniture, gathered from forgotten corners of the city, sat in the center of the club like remnants of a life left behind.

To Ember Lee's left, salvaged restaurant booths curved along the wall, their cracked vinyl patched with duct tape. Small groups huddled there, heads low, voices softer than the hum of the overhead lights. Even here, no one dared speak too loudly. Not where the world above still loomed, waiting for them to resurface.

Not seeing who she needed, Ember headed to the dining area. She wasn't exactly welcome with the Halfers, and wouldn't usually engage with them, but she wanted to finish up her business down here as quickly as possible. Choosing the four at the first booth, Ember eased toward them.

"Where's Chase?"

Two words. As quick a question as she could manage. One Halfer glared at her, and none of them answered.

Ember glanced over the nearby tables, sure they would have heard her. No one looked up or offered help. Nevermind that she'd been the catalyst who'd freed them a few days ago. As far as they were concerned, her existence was the root cause of all their problems.

Chase wasn't there, then, or at his house, which meant waiting. Tension coiled throughout Ember, her body filled with the need to escape, though there was no actual danger there. Turning her back on the unhelpful Halfers, Ember made her way to the kitchen, a galley style space with scavenged cabinetry along the back wall and a long, straight bar top that separated the cooking area from the rest of the Club.

The Club wasn't usually this crowded. In fact, it was supposed to be closed for the winter months, allowing the children full run of the place. The boxing ring where Keegan had trained Ember and the Halfers had been transformed into an infant and toddler area. The older kids had small beds lined up along where other exercise equipment had been removed.

It provided less space for the teens to occupy, but wandering topside wasn't a popular choice these days, after Charlah had come through Trifecta, capturing the minds and bodies of most of the Halfer population. Ember had broken that connection, but no one wanted to risk meeting her again.

Only she and Chase left the underground space. Ember couldn't be taken over by the Queen, which made her more suspicious in the Halfers' eyes. It didn't matter. She'd never been comfortable staying inside for long. Chase said he had work to do. Ember took the hope that this particular trip of his would be quick.

The seats at the kitchen bar were empty. She sat with her

back to the Halfers' glares and the children's noise. A squeal sliced through Ember's ears and she winced as it echoed off concrete walls and bounced along the high, gray ceiling.

Ember didn't hate little kids. They were just loud. There was no reason the sight of tiny creatures should result in a clenched jaw. The sound of their talking-over-each-other voices shouldn't have brought her shoulders closer to her ears.

Her vehement reaction was likely because of the verge-poor sleep she'd been getting the past few nights. Surely it had nothing to do with how her mother stood at the center of their chaos. Hair neatly combed, clothes without wrinkles. Caretaking. Smiling.

Susan had bloomed in her new position with the Halfers. It was as if, down here, she felt the threat of magic less. She'd found purpose while fulfilling an old dream, as Susan wished the outcasts had taken her and her daughter in seventeen years ago.

It was a good thing. Ember should be happy for her mom. And she was. It was simply because their joyful noise was high-pitched. That's why she wanted to plug her ears. It wasn't because she despised the sound of her mother engaging. Laughing.

Hate had to be too strong a word.

Hopefully.

"I'm tapping out." A soft voice, so familiar, Ember would know it anywhere. Words spoken in a tone so light, they might have come from a stranger.

Susan had called out for a break, letting her co-caretaker trade places. It was a perfect situation for them both. Susan was recovering from years of sickness and Nancy Powell was months into her pregnancy. Since she was underground, the child's father was likely a mage. Her family might have kicked her out, or she'd left before they had the chance. Either way, she partnered well with Susan as they could take turns engaging, then resting.

Ember reached for the stack of cups, their smoky, faded red blending into the faint lines of unreadable text. A pitcher rested next to the plastic tower, filled and set out because the water coming from the pipes was nearly too cold to drink. As she poured, Ember could sense her mother getting closer with every step. The nicks and scratches of the handle pressed into the skin of her palm as she gripped stronger than necessary.

When Susan settled in next to her at the bar, Ember nodded a hello, putting the pitcher down carefully. She took a sip of water, hoping the lukewarm liquid would cool the hot coal burning at the juncture of her ribs. Now that they both sat here, Ember heard the chatter behind them simmer to a low buzz and the itch of being watched bit between her shoulder blades. Not only did they distrust Ember, they were cautious of Susan, the only adult Chase had ever given access to the Underground.

"Hey, honey."

Susan's silver-streaked hair, usually so messy, had been brushed and tied into a simple low ponytail. Her clothes fit well, not twisted or wrinkled from days of wear. Her dark gray irises were unclouded, and even the circles beneath her eyes seemed brighter.

Ember downed the rest of her water, letting the heavy weight of her long black hair anchor the back of her head. Her lashes squeezed together to trap the extra moisture behind her lids.

Why was she like this? All Ember had ever wanted was for her mom to be healthy. Normal. It wasn't Susan's fault that being part of a community and having a purpose was exactly what she needed, or that the option hadn't existed for her until now.

Never mind that Ember, her daughter, should have been enough.

Ember gave up trying to get more water out of the emptied

cup. There wasn't enough liquid in the world to extinguish the fire in her gut.

"What do you have planned today?" Susan brushed a stray lock of hair over Ember's shoulder, leaving itchy goosebumps behind.

"I'm waiting for Chase." Hopefully, the sharp edges of her words came across as impatient.

"How is he doing?" Susan's question invoked a tragic three-day-old memory. Charlah had trapped Leona in her grip as Ember struggled with the idea of using her power in full view of the Coven's High Priestess. The debate had proven pointless the moment Charlah killed Leona. Chase's mother.

"As well as can be expected."

Susan sighed. "It's such a shame. I can't imagine how he's managing. And I wish I could have met the woman who created this."

Ember shook her head, fingers picking at the knitted cuffs of her rich brown sweater. Anything to keep her silver eyes down in case they might give away the dark emotions she worked to suppress.

"Leona only raised a few of them topside," Ember corrected. "Chase and the Halfers did all this."

"All of it? So it's not..." Susan's whispered words trailed off. She flattened her hands against the countertop, bracing them against her tremors. "Magic?"

"Nope." Chase appeared from behind them, wearing his long black coat. He pulled off his leather gloves, then his heavy hood. Red-gold hair grew unbrushed and wild atop his head. The bags under his eyes fell deep into his cheeks as he grabbed Ember's glass, then refilled it from the sink, frost coating the outside.

"There was enough to get started. A water line here, and the tunnel lighting gave us access to the solar grid. We scrounged from old campers and abandoned houses for everything else. Nothing to worry about, Susan. It's all human down here."

Except for the mixed blood, of course. But except for Chase, Halfers couldn't use magic, so it didn't matter.

"How are the kiddos?" Chase asked Susan, his stiff tone balanced between an old anger and a new acceptance. He wasn't quite over Ember's mom kicking her out a few weeks ago. After Charlah had destroyed her house, though, Chase did what he did best and took in an outcast. Now Susan was entrenched with his closest kept secret: the care of children literally left on empty doorsteps or deep in the forest, with no regard to whether or not they'd be found.

"Oh, they're wonderful." The lines around Susan's eyes deepened as her cheeks bubbled with her smile. She glanced over her shoulder to see them and Ember mimicked her motion. Nancy finished fixing a girl's hair, then leveraged herself upright with a hand at the small of her back.

"It's so nice for you to take us in." Susan clasped her hands in thanks. "How long have you known Ember?"

"I've been helping Chase for years. He's the one who's supplied us with food and clothes." Ember's tone started out reasonably, but sharpened with each word, the bitterness in the depths of her gut finding a small escape through her voice. She cleared her throat and reached for her cup, only to remember Chase had claimed it, ignoring how Susan blinked her eyes in rapid succession and how Chase's green gaze narrowed.

He'd just lost his mother for verge sake and here she was snapping at hers.

Time to leave before she made the situation worse.

"I have something to show you." Ember's rushed words were soft with breathlessness. Chase raised an eyebrow in her direction.

"And that is?"

Ember glanced at Susan, curling her lips between her teeth. With her eyes back on her hands, she shook her head.

"Ah." Susan pushed up from her stool. "Time to check in with Nancy. I'll see you later, honey."

Ember nodded, unsure Susan saw the gesture as quickly as she turned from the bar.

Chase was kind enough not to say anything as he washed up the cup he'd shared with Ember, then put it on the bottom of the stack.

"Go for a walk?" He gestured toward the mirror-covered door behind him, the only disguised one in a room that held ten other visible doors along the curved exterior. Ember jumped at the easy out he offered, grabbing the red puff coat she'd hung on the backrest.

"Yeah, but not that way."

Chase arched a brow but followed Ember's lead as she guided him toward an exit near the children's space—the one that opened by the entrance to what used to be her home with Susan. The door groaned softly as it closed behind them, sealing out the faint murmurs of the club.

Side by side, they ascended the sloping concrete tunnel, their footsteps the only sound echoing through the passage. The rectangular corridor stretched ahead, its edges softened by a thin layer of dust disturbed by their steps. Overhead, dim solar-powered lights flickered, embedded in the ceiling since the original construction. Their glow struggled to hold back the weight of the shadows pressing in from the corners.

The silence between them felt fragile, like it might crack under the strain of unspoken thoughts. The air carried a dry, metallic chill, and each breath left behind a faint taste of stone and old earth.

"Look." Chase examined her as if trying to judge what words to use based on her expression. "I can't imagine how you feel about your mom right now. It's just hard for me to stay mad at her after what happened to mine."

"I'm not mad at her," Ember insisted, her speech quick and sharp. More defensive than true.

Chase accepted her claim with a nod.

"Right. Well, whatever your reaction, just know I'm on your side. She did kick you out of your house."

Ember fisted her hands in the pockets of her coat and stopped in her tracks. Chase took another step before twisting to face her. The edges of her eyes strained as she held them wide and wild against Chase's narrowed gaze.

"Are you threatening to ban her from the underground? She's been helping. She hasn't—"

"Hey." Chase raised empty palms. "Calm down. I don't mean anything like that. Ember, please. Take this in the intended spirit. A friend saying it's okay, whatever 'it' is."

Ember looked away, hiding her discomfort behind eyes squeezed shut. With a deep breath, she forced relaxation into her body and resumed walking toward topside, hoping that what she was about to do would help her world turn right side up again, putting her on equal footing with her friend.

"Okay, thanks. And now there's something I can do for you. For the Halfers. Something that will make things better."

Chase stiffened. Was it surprise, or lack of trust? Maybe a bit of both, if he wondered how she had anything worth giving.

"What are you talking about?" he asked.

Ember sucked air through her nose and blew it out through pursed lips.

"It will be easier if I show you."

2

NICU

Nicu tightened his grip on the thick wooden beam, his fingers curling against the unyielding surface of the bed frame's high, simple canopy. The wood held firm, cool beneath his touch, as if resisting him. With his feet planted on the mattress and hands locked around the bar, Nicu closed his eyes, surrendering to the silence and the heavy press of darkness surrounding him.

The Fae Ink responded to his focus, sliding across his body like liquid shadow. Tattoos shifted along his torso, bottle-necking at his shoulders before spilling down his arms, darkening until they formed a full sleeve. The dense swirls of Ink, usually no more than a shade richer than his skin, now stood out, defying the room's absence of light.

He coaxed the Ink further, guiding it into his palms and over his fingers. It crept between his flesh and the wood, the rough grain beneath his grip softening into a smooth, silky texture. Inch by inch, the Ink pressed deeper, bringing him closer to mastering a skill he had only dared attempt once before.

A few months ago, Promise Magic almost broke when Ember Lee chose to interact with humans. The result was not one Nicu cared to entertain, and he'd been reckless. His tattoos had left his skin and pulled Ember free from the grip of the powerful Veil that surrounded Trifecta. It was an action considered impossible for most Fae. For those born to it, the skill was seen as a forbidden and dark form of Fae magic.

A pressure built within his room, the particles of air turning heavy with an activation of magic Nicu had not called on. Pausing his experiment, he tested the flow to see if someone nearby was casting a spell.

The power trace did not connect to another mage, but to himself.

The Promise Magic was a mistake from his childhood. A nine-year-old Fae who thought he could solve two problems with a forbidden piece of Fate Magic by exchanging his protection for Ember's departure from human society. Now it buzzed around him with the feeling of half-slumber. Had his exercise brought it to life? Or was Ember making decisions that alerted the forces of the universe?

Nicu released the beam, dropping to the mattress. The Ink slipped backward, swirls and curves one shade darker than his skin settling back into their resting places. He counted each inhale, sent out a longer exhale, examining the energy that flickered at the edge of his senses.

Was this a warning? A hint that working forbidden magic within the confines of Fae housing was only him daring to be caught? He did not want to defy the Fae, and never meant to disappoint them. Nicu recalled how difficult it was for the Gypsum-born Elders, how they struggled to regain strength lost during the Fade. How they came back stronger, putting rules in place to guard against outsiders learning their weaknesses, and from taking advantage.

He'd sworn to be the barrier they needed. To use his mutations to help them remain safe, to do the things that went against their own values. To keep his and Branna's positions secure as well.

Nicu refused to believe he had to choose between the Fae and the Trimarked Child, or that the balance he'd sought for his whole life was inevitably impossible. Granting her a Promise might have been a mistake, but it also allowed him the leverage needed to hold onto that belief.

Promise Magic had tried to claim its price before. When Nicu strayed too close to his loyalty to the Fae. When Ember struck out in rebellion, needing to find release from her restrictions. Nicu learned to redirect the Promise, to reassure it that his lean toward the Fae was to protect Ember, not avoid his duty. That Ember's irresponsible choices did not count because they were due to a lack of understanding and intention.

Nicu sat with legs crossed, his hands palm-up in his lap as he closed and opened his fingers. If this flare of Promise Magic was because of Ember and not a warning toward him, he needed more options. He'd saved her once before by manipulating his Living Ink. If he learned to control it, it may be the key to keeping her safe while allowing him to remain loyal to his people.

His door whipped open, the ornate handle digging into the wall where it hit. Corporeal shadows flooded the room. Light struggled to breach the doorway between the black shapes forging their way in. Nicu did not object as they wrapped around his wrists and ankles, pulling him into the main space of the suite.

Branna's dark brown eyes flared with tones of red. Her normally smooth top bun was askew, and her mauve lips pulled back to show bright white teeth of stark rage.

"What happened?" He kept his voice low and calm. There was no other way to interact with Branna in this mood.

"You and your precious hybrid girl have ruined everything."

Nicu checked once again on the sparks of Promise Magic, their appearance and Branna's grievance appearing too close together to feel like a coincidence. That they remained at low alert did not bring him peace, but allowed him to swallow any alarm.

"I need more information if you want me to understand."

"I will make you understand," she hissed, her voice curling like smoke through the room. Shadows slithered from her, wrapping around Nicu's body, seeping into his skin with a cold that bit deeper than winter air. The darkness pressed in, thick and absolute—swallowing light, sound, and even the faintest sense of space.

Yet, one thing pierced through.

Edan materialized before him, his figure sharp against the suffocating black. A deep frown creased his lips as his gaze shifted toward Branna, her eyelids narrowed with quiet judgment. Nicu's breath caught mid-chest, tight and unforgiving, as if the shadows had wrapped around his lungs. His eyes burned —not from the dark, but from the weight of truth that settled between them like an unwanted brand.

Branna's shadows unraveled, peeling away as if they had never truly been there, revealing the lush suite. Edan's image faded with them, dissolving into the air between them. Nicu stood frozen, his muscles stiff with the effort to remain still. To speak now would do nothing but confirm what Branna already knew.

Edan was dead, and Branna was right. Nicu had allowed Ember to grant Edan's request to leave Trifecta. His lieutenant was supposed to gather information from the outside and bring it back.

"Stop looking at me like that," she spoke through clenched teeth. "As if you care for someone other than your Trimarked Child."

"Branna."

The necromancer scowled at him and waved in the direction he'd seen Edan's form. Apparently, she wasn't willing to listen to either of them at the moment.

"How?" Nicu asked, not able to keep the hollow tone from his voice.

Branna's voice broke far more than his as she answered. "He Fell."

Nicu's knees weakened, nearly sending him to the floor. His hand gripped the doorframe as his thoughts fought to rise through a flood, wanting to focus on concrete options instead of the quagmire of useless emotion.

No. It was impossible. The Elders had spoken of the affliction, of how a Fae outside the realm of Gypsum lost their soul. Their bodies were cursed to wander the foreign land, searching and seeking to fill the void. They destroyed populations. Worlds. But the process was supposed to take decades, not weeks.

"Where is his body?"

"How the verge should I know? He is a new spirit and I rarely hear them as it is. And what would you do about it, Nicu? Follow him? Lose your own soul? Leave behind your precious ward?"

Nicu swallowed against the hope peeking through Branna's wide, desperate eyes as her words lashed him with the truth they both knew.

Edan was not Nicu's priority, even in death.

There were few moments he regretted his attachment to the Trimarked Girl. This would be one he remembered for the rest of his life.

A banging at the front door bounced off the tension strung between Nicu and Branna. Mated by the Fae but never each other's chosen one.

Branna sucked in a breath and banished her shadows. Nicu walked toward the entry but before he could unlock it, the door opened to reveal Council Elder Wist at the forefront with two Terraborn Fae, Altaya and Daz. Wist was draped in his formal wrap of light blues and deep purples, its distinct pattern a direct tie to his ancestors. Altaya wore flexible pants and a long-sleeved shirt, their leather jacket in their arms. Daz had found something in between, with pressed slacks and a button-down.

This was not a normal morning greeting. Nicu noted the worry in Daz's pale skin and the frustrated pinches around Altaya's deep brown eyes. It appeared they'd also been called without warning.

Wist eyed Nicu's shirtless state and Branna wrapped in a robe.

"Dress to go out."

Wist remained on the threshold. Nicu turned toward his suite to see Branna closing her door, showing more control than he thought she had by shutting it gently.

From his wardrobe, Nicu pulled on fur-lined pants and three layers of shirts. He grabbed his coat, as it wasn't likely he'd return anytime soon with a greeting such as this.

Wist led the group of four Terraborn Fae through the moon-glow enchanted halls. They exited through the hidden door at the back of a well-ordered garden shed that disguised the entrance of their underground living quarters. Above ground, they entered the courtyard between the old human cabins, now refurbished into workshops, kitchens, and decoy homes.

At the midpoint of the north side, a sprawling meeting hall loomed, its heavy logs darkened with age and polished to a quiet sheen. The Fae's finest artisans had transformed the structure, carving every inch with the haunting faces of deities and delicate silhouettes of the city skylines they had left behind in true Gypsum. The carvings seemed to shift in the faint light, their watchful eyes following those who approached.

Their small group crossed the threshold into the dim interior. The morning sun hung too low to breach the tall, narrow windows, leaving the room steeped in cool shadows that stretched long across the floor. Dust lingered in the air, illuminated by the flickering electric lanterns hanging from iron sconces.

Angled benches flanked the central aisle, their emptiness pressing in like watchful sentinels. The carpeted path led to a raised dais at the far end, where the full Council waited. The Elders sat still and wordless, their gazes cutting through the gloom as the group approached. Wist's seat stood empty at the center of the platform—silent and commanding, as if his presence lingered even in his absence.

"Sit," he ordered them, pointing to the front benches. Altaya and Daz took the right side. Branna slid in on the left, dressed in her signature black as a steady reminder of her necromancer powers. Her stiff form was the only sign she wasn't happy that Nicu sat next to her, yet that could be interpreted as her desire to be anywhere but here.

Wist climbed the three deep steps and took his place amongst the Council. Nicu scanned the faces of the Elders, all dressed in their formal decorative wraps, each woven with the distinctive patterns of their ancestral family. As if they'd all agreed on the same posture, their hands rested on the table before them, their facial features indifferent and secretive.

"What do you know of High Priestess Leona's death?" Wist asked, claiming control of the interview.

A question required a response. Though the reply should be simple, it wasn't. The inquiry presented new details, a piece of the puzzle he hadn't had three nights ago when he watched a blood covered Aaron walk with the Trimarked Child and her mother. Yet, he could not react. That would provide more information to the Elders than he wished to give. Nicu schooled his features flat and gave a crisp, clear answer without infliction that joined seamlessly with the matching answers chorused from the Terraborn.

"Nothing."

Wist's direct gaze shifted. This question would be for him alone, then.

"Where is Edan?"

Only Nicu's lifelong practice of control kept the flinch from his face. He hoped any reaction from Branna would be interpreted as her usual ire.

"You requested data to be collected on the humans."

Wist's eyes sharpened. Nicu had not worded his response correctly. His answer hadn't been a lie, but he'd left Edan out of the statement. It was a mistake he rarely made, and Wist had caught it.

"So he is investigating within Trifecta?" Wist asked.

Pointed. Glaring. Accusatory.

Nicu did not want to answer.

"Where else would he be?" Branna demanded with a huff. At least she still favored Nicu slightly more than the Elder. Of course, her reply was not a lie. Edan's spirit was, indeed, within Trifecta.

"In his investigations," Wist continued, "did he come across news of the High Priestess?"

"It is difficult to know about the Witches when you are studying humans."

Though Branna deflected, many Council members wore expressions suggesting they did not believe Edan wasn't aware. Edan was the greatest secret collector and keeper of the Terraborn generation. He'd also been covetous of that clandestine information, and unlikely to have briefed Nicu or Branna. Even when asked by the Elders, Edan's riddles hid a plethora of secrets. That truth would keep them safe for now.

"We have learned enough," Council Elder Ethna declared from Wist's direct right. Wist sat back in his chair, though the heavy heat of his gaze upon Nicu showed he was not satisfied. "When Edan makes contact, send him to one of us."

"Absolutely." Branna's voice was too sweet. Nicu's eyelids twitched. Wist's sudden stillness proved he noticed. Nicu drew in a deep breath to recenter himself.

"We are reassigning three of you," Council Elder Neyu

announced from Wist's left. Each of the Terraborn leaned forward to signal they were listening. Nicu breathed back arguments driven by a deep need to remind the Council that he was the Trimarked Child's guardian, a position he'd been told took precedence.

"It should have escaped no one's attention that the Chaos Star still rules the sky, and for weeks longer than usual," Neyu continued. "As always, we have been on guard against the forces of Fate and Chaos as they try to force the Fae into subservience, and have marked the High Priestess's death and the humans' behavior shifts as bad omens for the Fae. We must become more proactive."

The Elders granted their audience a moment to register the gravity of the news. Fate and Chaos were forces to be resisted. Ember's birth was proof of their meddling, a mark of disruption woven into the realm's fragile balance. It was this very truth that made Nicu's mission to control her paramount to Fae safety.

It was also why his use of Promise Magic had earned him the disdain of many Fae. Any use of Fate Magic was strictly forbidden. At least they didn't know he'd gone so far as to grant a Wish.

Elder Ethna leaned forward, signaling her turn to speak.

"The High Priestess was the primary liaison between mages and humans, and there is no obvious replacement within the Coven. We will have to put in more effort. We shall send Daz and Branna to Town as our representatives."

Branna stiffened, and Nicu wondered if the source was irritation or pleasure. She'd longed to be relieved of guarding the Trimarked Child, but perhaps this was not the assignment she envisioned. The pairing made sense from the Council's point of view. Daz was a friendly and familiar Fae to the humans, as he ran a booth at the Saturday markets. Branna was their most formidable Fae and would present an implicit reminder that they were well defended.

"Nicu, you shall partner with Altaya and their hunting party," Council Elder Neyu ordered. "Altaya, you and your team are to act as cover for Nicu, who will be keeping watch for signs of human movements, and aide him as needed. The gulls have increased their presence in the forest because of their search for the Halfers. The humans should not find them, or evidence of them, lest the Remembrance Spell continue to be tested. It is your job to ensure they remain within its control."

Nicu nodded his agreement, a mixture of emotion traveling his spine. His assignments always focused around ensuring Chaos did not infect Center. Regardless of Wist's opinions at the moment, this was a legitimate application of Nicu's role for the Fae.

Testing the air, Nicu noted the Promise Magic had faded during the morning. Whatever had caused it, him or Ember, the threat had dissipated. He could dedicate this time to the Fae without guilt, to help keep the tenuous balance between the races of Trifecta while keeping his promises and fulfilling his purpose. No matter how the magic shifted, Nicu found comfort in the warm pressure of the medallion hidden in his braids, his newest connection to Ember even when she was out of sight.

3

BRANNA

"Branna, a word."

Branna paused in her steps, somewhat grateful for the excuse it gave her to not to follow directly on Nicu's heels as he left the building.

About time for a fading break.

Without it, Branna might have killed him — sending him to join Edan. The dead Fae had lingered at her side since his arrival that morning, his form flickering like a shadow caught between worlds. He barely had the strength to tell her what happened.

His soul had been ripped from his still-living body, torn apart by the lack of Gypsum's energies outside the Veil. His mission to gather information hadn't simply failed — it unraveled in the worst possible way, leaving his body to wander aimlessly while his spirit anchored itself to her, bound to haunt her for the rest of her days.

On second thought, maybe she wouldn't kill Nicu after all. The idea of being tethered to his ghost felt worse than the Trimarked babysitting missions she already despised. Death would be too easy for him.

Branna wanted him to suffer. To understand the ache that

hollowed her chest and burned her throat every time Edan's ghost flickered into view. Let Nicu know what it was like to be haunted by loss at every turn—just as she was.

Branna turned to find the council members had risen from their seats as they chatted in low voices. Wist descended to the lower floor, stopping only a few feet from her.

"This way." Wist directed her out of the aisle. Branna followed him past the long bench until they reached the outer wall. Her new partner, Daz, spoke with Elder Ethna, his posture erect and his cheeks flush as he hung on her every word. His desire to leave the weaving hut left him willing to engage with humans for the break. His emotions echoed how she felt about being separated from Nicu. For an actual job at that.

Giving the necromancer real responsibility was not how the Fae operated. They might have wanted to isolate her and Nicu, but they were more likely to send her back to her rooms than reassign her. Sure, she acted as the 'bad Fae' to Daz's 'good,' but it was possible for a bow-carrying Terraborn to serve the same purpose.

So what did they want?

Branna shaped her expression into careful boredom, leaving just enough emotion to avoid suspicion. She had long since mastered the art of showing others exactly what she wanted them to see. The Fae dismissed her as reckless, lacking the discipline of the Elders—and she let them.

Their underestimation served her well. They could assume she was impulsive, driven by passion rather than precision. It made them overlook the sharpness behind her eyes, the quiet calculations ticking away beneath the surface. While they believed she lacked control, Branna watched and listened, her suspicions about their new assignments growing with each passing moment.

Welcome or not, she intended to uncover the truth.

"I assume you've seen this evidence of humans breaking out of our compulsion?" Wist asked.

Branna nodded in response. Brandt had been the first of the gulls to slip free from the Fae's dampening spell, the enchantment designed to keep humans from lingering on thoughts of mages. Stumbling into power he couldn't grasp had shattered him. In the end, it killed him.

Then there was Aaron. Each day spent with the Halfers and the Trimarked girl sharpened his awareness. Unlike Brandt, Aaron seemed to accept magic easily, but that didn't make him less dangerous.

These two were outliers, but their connection to mages and the Chaos Star shouldn't be ignored. They might be the first signs of something worse—a ripple in the magic that kept human minds veiled. If more gulls broke free, it may signal a weakness in the Remembrance Spell. Perhaps the Council's sudden interest in abandoned children wasn't driven by conscience, but by fear of losing the upper hand.

"I have a concern that extends beyond the humans. I would bring it up with Nicu, but he has become exceptionally skilled at keeping things from me."

Was that pride in Wist's voice? An accidental slip or a purposeful attempt at manipulation? A reminder that he considered her lacking. She would save her eye roll for later, after he finished wasting her time.

"I worry that our binding on the Child may also be waning. Have you noticed anything about her behavior? Has she been trying to slip away from you more than usual?"

"The Trimarked Child is completely aware that she cannot 'slip by' one of the Fae," Branna countered, mostly because she was tired of hearing the Elder's voice. Finding and guarding Ember had been easy, part of the reason for Branna's boredom over the last decade.

Wist stood in silence for a moment, the conniving Elder likely weighing which words would best suit his needs. Branna needed to be careful. The Elder always saw more than intended. She surreptitiously made sure her tattoos covered the light gray marks on her skin. They had grown along with her powers, yet were small enough to hide beneath the Living Ink of her scythe-shaped tattoos.

If he discovered the anomaly, Wist would decide to keep her in Center. What he did with her after that was best pushed from her imagination.

"I encourage you to judge your answer well. If our bindings are losing their potency, it makes sense to contain the Trimarked Child. For our safety and the rest of Trifecta."

The edges of Branna's vision darkened, the room narrowing into a tunnel of seething heat. How dare he speak to her of containment? His words scraped like gravel, every syllable a reminder of the past he had no right to mention.

He was the one who tried to kill Ember, casting a spell meant to snuff out a life before it had barely begun. Instead, his failure cost Branna her own, scarring her soul and twisting her into what she became. And then he walked away, leaving an infant to carry the unbearable weight of his shame.

Let them all rot in the void. Branna's jaw tightened until it ached. She was done pretending they could play house together.

"I haven't seen anything."

Truth. It was one of Nicu's rules to guard without seeing. Wist had made a mistake when he failed to ask for knowledge. Not that Branna would have given him that, either.

As a necromancer, not fully Fae, she could lie.

"Perhaps your spirits, then?" Wist asked.

"It's difficult for me to hear them. When they get a chance to talk, they are selfish creatures, only speaking about what matters to them."

"What is selfish is allowing a dangerous creature to go unchecked and unchallenged."

Wist returned her criticism in kind, a reminder that her own power was nearly as feared as Ember's. But the Elder did not deserve Branna's loyalty, and she had her own grievances to unleash on the Trimarked Child.

"Ember is harmless."

"That is still up for debate. Interesting that you seem to find it otherwise."

This was why secrets mattered. The Elder was completely unaware that Branna had discovered her connection to Ember —nor that her power had surged when Nicu nearly triggered the Trimarked medallion, breaking a bond the Fae never thought to mention. Through the artifact, some magical thread tied Branna to Nicu and Ember, and when it frayed, her strength bloomed.

The tear was worth it. Branna's grip over shadows sharpened with each passing day. In true darkness, spirits appeared as vividly as the living. Even in the light, their gentle energy signatures hovered around her, brighter the younger their ghost. Though faint, Edan's presence held steady in a way souls had never manifested before.

For a brief moment, Branna wondered if Edan sensed what Wist concealed beneath his careful words. But there would be no lowering her shadows to grant Edan voice and form—not after Wist's pointed warning about her gifts.

"Are you ready?" Daz's sudden appearance dissipated the signs of Edan's presence. The young Fae's excitement ignored the tension between Wist and Branna, leaving him unaware that he'd just invaded an Elder's space uninvited.

Wist accepted his intrusion with thin lips and a slight step away, signaling the official end of their conversation.

With a sigh directed at Daz, Branna flicked her fingers toward the exit as an invitation for him to lead the way.

"Report back to me." Wist raised his voice to a public volume, setting the expectation that they would meet later.

Branna ignored him, letting the heavy wooden door close between her and the Council.

Good luck finding a necromancer who doesn't want to be found.

4

EMBER

"An interesting choice of location."

Chase's words barely registered as Ember stared up at the hulking tree before them. It wasn't as tall as the towering redwoods nearby, but its trunk dwarfed them—twice the girth of the giants surrounding the barren stretch of No Man's Land.

For as long as Ember could remember, nothing had grown there. This place, caught at the crossroads of mage and human energies, devoured life. Trees that toppled within the boundary crumbled to dust, while those that fell just outside decayed slowly, draped in moss and threaded with fungi. The soil lay bare—no insects stirring beneath the surface. Even the sky seemed forsaken. No birds crossed the air above.

And yet, somehow, Tristan—rogue Wizard, deceiver, and her father—had defied the land's hunger. He planted this seed, fed it with souls, and raised this twisted colossus faster than her world had fallen apart.

"I've seen this before," Chase assured her. "A live tree in a dead space. Have you figured out why it's here?"

"I'm working on it, but this is about something else. Just look at it."

Chase stepped forward and Ember gripped his sleeve.

"No." The sharp whip of the word brought Chase up short, and he eased back. Ember wasn't sure how this thing ate souls, but she had a clear memory of its roots chasing after her in the cave directly beneath them. Only her power had stopped them from making contact long enough for her to escape with Devi and Aaron.

Ember called up the magical energy within her, coating her skin with a pale blue light. She extended the shield to flow over her hand to coat Chase in his own barely-there shell.

"What—?" Chase jerked back. Ember's gasp accompanied the small rasping friction from where they'd been connected. "What is this?"

Chase held his fingers in a beam of weak morning sunshine. His skin bore a pale blue sheen that faded away. A frown cut deep into his face.

"Wait. It's gone."

"It's not," Ember assured him. She tapped his shoulder and a small circle of blue appeared for only a second.

"What is it?"

"My power," Ember whispered, her heart pounding in her chest, leaving her light-headed as she met his gaze with wide, dry eyes.

This was trust. This was stupid, but she wanted to protect him from the tree. He was … he was a friend.

"Magic isn't visible."

"It's not magic." Her hands shook under his scrutiny and she tucked them under her arms. "It's Veil energy."

Chase didn't ask her how she knew, or how it was possible. He'd seen her manipulate the Veil for years while doing favors for him and the Halfers. He'd been there when the electric power of the barrier surrounding Trifecta had swallowed her whole. Still, his cheeks paled, and he looked away from her earnest gaze to search the forest.

"Ember," Chase murmured, "the mages could see you.

We're right on the Fae and Witch borders. Nicu could be watching. Why take the risk?"

A deep shudder rattled Ember's bones, the cold biting through her coat and settling in places she couldn't shake. The air, thin and sharp at this altitude, tasted like ice as it scraped down her throat. She forced the instinctive apprehension aside, clenching her hands to keep them steady. Getting caught wasn't an option.

They thought her power was sealed by the Ink etched into the back of her neck, a magical tattoo meant to bind her. Nicu, her ever-watchful Fae guardian, had drilled the warning into her over the years. *"Never forget, little hybrid, the Fae are the reason you're alive. They can change their minds."*

His voice echoed in her head, mingling with the memory of a Fae who drew too close not long ago. Ember imagined the weight of their gaze, the tension in the air as they approached —bow raised, arrow nocked and aimed at her heart. They hadn't seen her practicing her talent, but it had been a narrow escape.

Now, standing beneath the towering redwoods, their branches skeletal against the pale sky, Ember felt certain no eyes lingered on her, Fae or Witch. The forest lay still, the hush before snowfall pressing in on all sides. Yet she couldn't explain that certainty to Chase.

Instead, she did what she always did; ignored his questions and gave him the answer he was expecting.

"My shield will let you get near the tree safely. Look right there."

Ember pointed toward a break in the bark. It was hard to see, especially from a distance. A circle the size of a golf ball winked as a slow beam of the rising sun eased over it.

"What is it?"

"It's the gem Charlah wore around her neck."

Chase met Ember's eyes, searching them for something. Possibly honesty, or to judge her level of certainty.

"I got really close to it," she answered his silent probing.

Chase approached the tree but remained outside of touching of distance as he studied the smooth stone.

"You're sure?"

"Yes," Ember insisted. "It's a feeling, but not an emotional one."

"Magic." Chase stepped back to Ember's side, his shoulders squared and chin lifted, all signs of doubt gone. "I know a little about that."

"Because of Leona."

Ember winced as the name escaped her lips. She hadn't meant to bring up Chase's mother, with her loss still fresh enough to sting. But the truth lingered, heavy and unavoidable. Leona's teachings allowed Chase, a Halfer, to learn spell work. No other Halfers could wield magic. At least, no one would willingly teach them how to push past the limitations of their human blood.

But Chase stood apart. As the High Priestess's son, Leona shaped him into someone capable of leading the Halfers, the unwanted youth of Trifecta left with nowhere else to go. She had trusted him with that burden.

But now wasn't the time to open that wound.

"I'm sorry."

"No, you're good." Chase sighed. "You can't remind me she's dead. It's something that's always there."

Ember nodded, because she didn't know what else to say.

"What does this mean?" Chase redirected the conversation toward the gem.

"Do you remember how Devi told us the Queen was an experiment? Too many souls in one body. This crystal helped by holding them separate, but still close."

"Weird."

Ember agreed, but that wasn't the point. "My guess is that my father succeeded, and the tree ate her."

"Your father?" Chase's eyes pinned her.

"Don't we all have one? Turns out, mine returned. He brought Brandt back after I threw him out, and then somehow got Charlah in."

"How fading passable is this impenetrable barrier around Trifecta?" Frustration ground through Chase's words.

"It was that knife Brandt stabbed Aaron with," Ember answered. "But Charlah broke it."

"So you're still our only out."

A shudder trickled down Ember's spine and she fought her frown with a scowl. Not what she wanted to be known for.

Chase's lips thinned and he narrowed his eyes at the tree. She waited for him to ask her for more details, like how had she learned this? Where was Tristan now? She shifted between her feet, an odd crawly sensation spreading throughout her body.

"What does your father want?"

Other than me?

"I'm not sure."

Chase tilted his head back to gauge the tree's height.

"Aaron hasn't left his house for days."

"What?" Ember startled. "Even for school?"

"Not even for a run," Chase confirmed. "He should be told we're safe from Charlah."

"I didn't know. I can tell him —"

"Let me do it." Chase regained his natural posture and pulled on his hood. "I'll take him coffee this morning after his dad leaves. It'll give me something nice to look forward to."

Ember breathed through the tightness in her chest. While she was happy Chase was taking on this task, she realized she should find Aaron soon. She'd been so mad at him before when he'd been talking to everyone but her. She didn't want him to think she was avoiding him.

"Say hi for me."

Chase tilted his head toward her, popping out a sharp laugh.

"He'll think I'm lying if I tell him you said that."

Ember's lips quirked. "Then remind him it's his fault for starting this whole friend thing."

"Now that he might believe." Chase put his hands in his pockets and turned his back to the tree. "Are you heading in yet?"

Ember thought about laughing children in the underground space. How Susan played with them. How she and Nancy supported each other in ways Ember had never managed for her mom, or Susan for her.

"No."

"Okay. Be careful, then. And take these." Chase handed her the same gloves she'd refused to accept a few days ago. "Say you're borrowing them, or that you owe me a favor. Whatever you need to wear them and keep from getting frostbite."

Ember accepted the gloves without a word. Chase didn't move until she pulled them on. They fit her, meaning they were too small for him. She nodded in thanks, but couldn't meet his eyes.

"I want to say it will get better with your mom," Chase offered.

"Same."

Chase hummed in reluctant acknowledgement as he slipped on his deep, oversized hood. His footsteps crunched their way through the forest toward the Halfer Zone. Apparently, he had coffee to make before heading into Town.

"You did well with him."

That voice slithered through the air, slick and unwelcome. Ember's teeth clenched, but she turned to face it anyway.

Tristan Glynn leaned casually against a tree at the boundary of No Man's Land, one shoulder pressed into the rough bark. The massive trunk dwarfed his long, thin frame, but it did nothing to diminish the weight of his presence. His gem-like green eyes gleamed through the shadow of his black trilby, sharp and watchful, cutting through the distance between them. Everything about him—his slick clothes, his too-calm posture—felt like the edge of a knife hidden beneath silk.

Ember's pulse quickened. She pursed her lips and stepped back without thinking, ignoring the way her heel hovered dangerously close to the exposed roots of the soul-eating tree behind her.

She knew the Fae weren't nearby because of him. Tristan had kept watch while she showed Chase Charlah's crystal—the price of a deal she intended to collect.

"Great. Thanks for your approval. Now tell me everything."

Tristan's mouth curled into a sharp, angled smile, and the glint in his eyes promised he had far more to say than she'd bargained for.

5

AARON

"*D*ad, no more medicine. That Witch stuff tastes cruel."

Aaron lay curled on his side, sinking deeper into the full-sized bed as if the thick blankets shielded him from the world pressing in. His head tucked beneath the covers, his back toward the room—an illusion of safety he wasn't sure he believed but didn't release.

Three runs missed. A strength workout ignored. Two days of school skipped. But the weight that pinned him to the mattress never lifted. His relentless thoughts circled, whispering reminders he couldn't escape.

Trapped. Drowning in Charlah's power. Helpless as his body refused to obey.

A tree, unnaturally tall for something so newly sprouted, fed on the soul of a boy Aaron had known since fourth grade.

Brandt's soul.

Aaron braced for the familiar sting—the sharp slice of despair, the hollow ache of loss, the cold spin of fear. But nothing came.

Instead, there was only numbness, and somehow that felt

worse. He missed the pain. The emptiness sat heavy in his chest, and he wondered if grief would find its way back.

But after days of lying in bed, his dad had grown worried enough to seek out a Witch brew, as he called it, and poured it down Aaron's throat. He guessed it was working, then.

Clack-clack.

"Dad, I said no."

Rattlerattlerattle.

Wait. That wasn't Gus knocking at the door.

Aaron yanked down the blanket, twisting toward the window where the annoying sound originated. Gentle, gray light seeped in around the dark curtain. For the first time in days, it didn't hurt his head.

The rattling on the glass continued. Aaron crawled out of bed. He allowed himself one long, whole body stretch, the pops and cracks of his joints easing stiff muscles and stuck emotions.

Out the window, Aaron spotted Chase standing in the hibernating grass of his backyard, actual pebbles in his hands. When he saw Aaron, he dropped them and bent to pick up two insulated mugs he'd balanced between his feet, lifting one up in offering.

The day was suddenly infinitely better. Chase's visit must mean it was a safe moment. Relief gave Aaron the space to grin and wave back, then let the curtain drop. With quick movements, he pulled off his sleeping shirt, only to gag at the stench.

He could not meet Chase smelling like rotten cheese.

Aaron rushed to the bathroom after grabbing an armful of random but clean clothes. With his stuff plopped in the sink, he cranked on the shower and jumped in, yelping at the still-freezing water. He didn't let the temperature stop him from getting washed up and was out in record time, eager to pull on his warm sweats and hoodie.

Using less care than normal, Aaron towel dried his caramel curls as much as possible and dropped the cloth on his way out. His jacket, knitted hat, and boots were stored next to the back door, and he stepped into them as he left the house.

"Hey." Aaron grinned, thankful he didn't sound out of breath after his mad rush.

Chase smiled in greeting, handing out a dented and scratched metal tumbler, complete with a plastic lid. There weren't many of these in Trifecta. A relic from pre-Convergence days, the Witches didn't recreate them as they did clothing or medicines. Of course, Chase had some, though; the guy was smart and frugal.

"Haven't seen you in a while, so I thought I'd bring coffee to you. You alright?"

"Oh." Aaron looked at his cup and carefully slid open the mouthpiece. That Chase was checking on him was a fist to the gut.

"Dude, I'm fine. You, though, how are you?"

"Don't do that," Chase snapped, and then took a deep breath. "I can't … I can keep it together, but only if you don't ask me that. We good?"

"Yeah. Sorry."

"Stop. This isn't about me." Chase looked across the connected backyards with a frown. The Halfer Zone had houses separated by fencing, but here, no barrier existed between the properties. With a jerk of his chin, Chase directed them back to the tree line.

Aaron hesitated, staring at the spaces between the trees, looking for a cap of long platinum hair, or a flash of a shimmering green dress. Chase was halfway across the yard before he noticed Aaron's feet glued to the paved patio.

"It's okay," Chase soothed. "Come on, I want to explain."

Aaron shook with each step toward the redwoods. His house was on human lands. Charlah wasn't interested in humans. The forest was closer to No Man's, closer to mage lands. The conviction that Chase was safe allowed Aaron to follow.

Coffee splashed through the small opening in the lid, scalding Aaron before cooling into a sticky film against his skin. By the time he reached Chase, his hands trembled, slick with the spill. Aaron's eyes stayed unfocused, staring somewhere past the ground as though the world had narrowed to a tight tunnel around him.

Chase took the cup gently, his grip steady against Aaron's shaking fingers. Without a word, he pulled his wool sleeve down, cleaning off Aaron's hands like it wasn't the first time this had happened. The small gesture grounded Aaron for a moment, but the cold dread still clung to him, sticky and persistent — just like the coffee.

"Aaron, I came to tell you that you're safe," Chase murmured. "Charlah is gone."

"What?"

Light rushed back into Aaron's vision. He jerked his attention from the vague nothingness of the ground to meet Chase's unshaken gaze.

"How do you know?"

"Ember. She said she can't explain it, but that she knows Charlah is gone. Something to do with that tree."

Nausea rose up. Aaron breathed deep through his nose to counteract it.

That fading tree.

At least it took someone he hated this time.

"Here. Take your coffee." Chase put the mug back in Aaron's grip. "Let's talk about anything else."

Aaron chuckled, happy with Chase's suggestion.

"Aaron?"

Chase and Aaron stepped deeper into the forest, both refocusing toward the Harwell house. Paul had opened the back door and frowned into the outside space.

"Verge. I must have left a trail."

"PJs and hygiene products?" Chase asked.

Aaron laughed and ran a hand through his damp, slightly

frozen hair, cheeks flushed at being called out. He lifted the tumbler to his lips to muffle the sound so it wouldn't reach Paul.

"Something like that. I should go." Aaron shifted his weight from one leg to the other, then handed Chase his coffee stained mug.

"Nah. Keep it. You can return it later when you're done."

Chase gestured toward the house while giving Aaron a wink, then he made his way through the trees, careful to stay out of sight.

Paul had moved out onto the patio and curved his hands around his mouth to act as an amplifier.

"Aaron!"

Aaron flinched at the first loud noise he'd heard in days. With a sigh, he lifted one heavy boot after the other back toward his old teammate and the previous soccer captain. Though Paul had graduated from school the year before, they caught up every week or so. Gus must have told him Aaron had been sick.

"Hey, Paul." Aaron waved on his way in, a greeting and an acknowledgment that he'd heard his friend's shout. "What are you doing here?"

"I came to see your dad. He said you were home again. Looks like you're improving?"

"Yeah. I woke up late, but better. Thought I'd get some fresh air."

"So that's why you missed the meeting?"

Aaron's lips flattened at Paul's tight tone. Paul liked to think his straightforward questions hid his emotions, but he never could keep frustration or disappointment from his voice. He reached the back door and led Paul into the warm kitchen, where they took off their boots and coats.

"What meeting?"

"Your dad didn't tell you? It's why I'm here. We're going to —"

"Leave him out of this. He's sick, Paul." Gus came into the kitchen dressed in slacks and a button-down, his usual outfit for when he taught high school math. Aaron stopped in his tracks. He hadn't thought to check for his dad before he'd gone out to meet Chase. Had he seen him go out?

"I'm better." Aaron studied Gus' level of distraction as he made instant coffee. He paused, likely to ask Aaron if he wanted any, but raised a brow at the tumbler.

So he probably hadn't spotted Chase, but he definitely noticed the mug, which he would have never seen before. Great.

"We addressed the lost kids," Paul shared. Aaron frowned, remembering how hot Paul had gotten a few days ago when they'd talked about the missing pregnant girl. How the town market had been quieter than usual. Now, there was even a meeting?

Does Nicu know?

Aaron hid his flinch behind taking a sip. Was it okay that first his thought was of the Fae? Should he worry more about the humans? It wasn't like the Halfers were in danger. At least, not at the moment.

"It's a bunch of parents who are suddenly growing a conscience," Gus muttered.

"Late or not, they're caring now. Which is why it's important for Aaron to be part of this," Paul argued. "One of the missing kids is his best friend."

Aaron tilted the cup higher, careful not to spill as he used the motion to hide more of his face and any expression that might try to slip through. He let the hot, rich liquid seep in and focused on the momentary distraction.

Ah. Chase's coffee was outstanding.

"Paul, give it a rest." At the sound of Gus's coaching voice, Paul dropped his eyes. A diploma didn't end a players' relationship with the sports coach he'd had for four years.

Gus moved to the island, fixated on the drink in Aaron's hand. "Other friends checked in on you this morning?"

"W-what?"

Aaron squirmed, not sure what Gus meant or how to tell him about Chase. Or Ember. Or anything that had happened since Brandt disappeared. Keeping secrets had never been a problem before. Aaron even came clean about the End of the World parties. Gus would grunt about teenage brains making teenage choices, then warn Aaron to be careful.

"Boy or girl?"

Aaron sputtered at his father's question. They were officially in new territory. Paul hid a snicker behind his hand.

"Sure you've been sick for three days?" his friend teased. "Should we check the other kids' school attendance?"

At least they still assumed he'd be dating a classmate. Because who else would he be seeing?

"Not ready to spill, yet?" Gus guessed. "Suppose that's fair."

Gus claimed the bar stool next to the one draped with Paul's coat. A heavy sigh sunk his shoulders, and he rubbed his face in his hands.

"I was hoping you'd be more sick," Gus spoke through his fingers, and Aaron choked on his coffee.

"Are you good, Coach?" Paul asked.

"Yeah. Sure. I need to get to work, but the town is going crazy right now. Even the teachers' lounge is full of talk about mages and missing kids. I'm tired of it. Probably took it out on you, Paul. Sorry."

"It's okay, Coach."

"Hmm." Gus nodded to Paul in thanks, then side-eyed Aaron's drink. "Lemme."

Gus reached out to Aaron, who handed over his tumbler. His dad had a taste, then grunted while looking at the dried spill lines coating the black sides.

"Whoever your friend is, they make good coffee." He stole

another sip, then considered Paul and Aaron. "Well, since I can't bury my head on this one. Paul, you've been asking questions. Did you discover anything?"

"Only more rumors," Paul grumbled.

"And Aaron," Gus redirected. "What about your search?"

"I didn't find anything out of the ordinary running around Town." It was not a lie. Everything strange occurred on Witch land or in Halfer territory. And he hadn't 'found' Brandt. Charlah had told Aaron what happened.

Brandt being eaten by a tree wasn't something Aaron could explain, even to his dad. Aaron drooped, supporting himself on the counter. Gus cared about the missing kids, but might care about Brandt more. He had worked to keep the kid busy with sports and away from an alcoholic father with a heavy fist.

"What do you boys know about the old flood system that runs under the city?" A surprised silence followed Gus's question.

"Oh, no." Paul shook his head. Aaron held his breath. "Kids dare each other to go into the tunnels all the time. They've never come across anything."

"I used to be one of those kids," Gus agreed. "And dare or not, but we didn't get very far in. I doubt that's changed, right?"

Aaron mimicked Paul's shake of the head.

"The structure is more than tunnels," Gus explained. "They used to channel spring melt into a huge holding tank. The city accessed the water in dryer months. We haven't needed the system since, well, probably my grandfather's time. It was twenty-five years ago or so when we sealed up the intake drains after a few kids got stuck in them. There are other access points, though, meant for maintenance. One just up the hill, actually, where the Lees live."

Where they used to live, before Charlah destroyed their house.

"I need more coffee." Aaron reclaimed his mug, needing

something to hide his face behind, a task to keep his hands occupied and to redirect nervous energy from his legs.

The Halfers were not ready for this. Most of them were still adjusting after having their bodies taken over. Chase had buried his mother and couldn't even be asked how he was doing.

Aaron wasn't prepared, either. He'd been the Queen's second victim and her favorite brain to shuffle through since he'd visited the Witches' Circle. She'd offered to make him her consort, a thought that still induced bile to burn the back of his throat.

Aaron leaned on the island, his head light and his chest heavy, the offset weights messing with his balance. He grabbed an apple from the bowl at the center of the countertop, then slipped onto the bar stool for support. Paul watched him, brow creased, likely concerned Aaron wasn't fully recovered.

"What's the plan, then?" Aaron asked. He didn't want to be involved. He needed to be.

"Paul," Gus said, "you know Janice, don't you? Council Secretary?"

"Yeah."

"She'll have a good idea on where to find the blueprints for those tunnels and where the keys for the access points are. Would you run down to the police station and ask her to look right away? Best to get this stuff done before people are out of work."

"Got it, Coach." Paul squeezed Aaron's shoulder on his way out, passed through the dining room and exited through the front of the house.

Any relief Aaron felt over learning he had at least a little time while Paul did his job was suppressed beneath the dread threatening to burn a hole through his chest. The situation was growing, and fast. Where it wasn't great how the Halfers came to be, they existed as their own community now. There was some sort of situational acceptance.

Trifecta had been a bury-our-heads kind of city for as long as Aaron remembered. Mostly, it meant each of the races stuck together, and that included the Halfers, once they were established. Keeping the peace in a place no one could escape had extended to ignoring certain circumstances. A woman wasn't seen for nearly a year, then returned with signs of pregnancy, but without a baby. People ignored evidence of family abuse, and some of those kids disappeared, too.

Chase didn't let anyone fall through the gaps. He adopted the abandoned and the escapees. He protected them, kept them from the topsiders while giving them ways to strike back with petty theft and minor pranks. It was a broken system, sure, but one that worked. If Gus pushed forward with this plan to find the missing kids, it could start an uncontrolled fire that would rage through the Underground, upsetting every slice of peace Chase had carved out for the Halfers.

It wouldn't stop there, either, likely burning Ember alive. She'd been through hell, some of it because of Brandt. Aaron had to help his dad calm things down on the human side. Maybe get him and Chase to neutral territory to talk before any doors were broken down.

Hope bubbled in Aaron as he imagined a peaceful negotiation, one that led to the Halfers not needing to hide anymore. That maybe they could come topside and be accepted. But that wouldn't work if their first encounter started with brute force.

"Dad—" he began, but Gus cut him off.

"Aaron. This friend of yours, it's not the Trimarked Child, is it?"

Aaron coughed and pounded his chest, pretending it was caused by a rogue piece of fruit and not his fear. Gus's question knocked all offensive thoughts from his head, leaving him unexpectedly on the defense.

"Dad."

"Look, son." Gus twisted in his chair and leaned in. Aaron

automatically put his twice bitten apple on the counter and straightened up to attention.

"I want to sit here and tell you it doesn't matter. That love is love. But..." Gus broke eye contact and ran a hand through his thick hair.

"The Trimarked Child is different. She's dangerous. Being with her, in any way, is risky. Even if she doesn't sprout magic, the mages watch her like a ticking bomb. You don't want to be anywhere near that kind of scrutiny, believe me."

"Yeah," Aaron nodded. "I get it."

"I really hope so."

Gus shook out his body as if at the end of a deadlift, shaking out the stress in his muscles. "That said. What's their name?"

"Dad!" Aaron rolled his eyes at his parent's attempt to dig some information out of him. Gus laughed and Aaron dodged a good-natured jab.

"Okay, then. Guess I'll get to the school to tell them I'm taking the day off. I really want to nip this whole line of questioning in the bud before a mob starts."

Gus leaned in to give Aaron a hug, missing the way Aaron's color bled from his face, or attributing it to his son's illness.

"Glad you're feeling better, son. Still, take it easy for a bit more. Maybe we can get back to things tomorrow."

"Yeah," Aaron agreed, and then watched his father walk out the door, no longer looking forward to when he returned the coffee tumbler to Chase.

6

EMBER

"The tree only ate half the Queen's souls."

Ember grit her teeth at Tristan's revelation, a detail he'd left out over the past few days when he'd cornered her a few times to interest her in helping. Something she was already regretting.

"Lies so soon," she snapped.

"Oh, Charlah's was one of them. You can feel good about what you told your friend."

"And the other half of her souls?"

"I'm certain that none of them will bother you. They wouldn't risk being added to the cause."

Tristan strode to the tree, his sharp lines softening as he placed a gentle hand against the bark. Ember eased away from both of them.

"Omissions are still lies. I just told Chase—"

"You explained the important parts and no more. Exactly like we planned." Tristan spun on his heels, a perfect about-face. His fierce gaze pinned her where she stood halfway between the tree and the Fae boundary.

"Might it help to know that I wish I'd done things differently? As a father, I mean."

"What the verge are you talking about?"

"Seeing the result of my choices, I'd have liked to stay behind. Raised you to embrace your purpose and understand my tactics. No one would have marked you or mistreated you."

The picture Tristan painted with his oily words left Ember with a strong urge to scrub them from her mind.

"You would have brainwashed me."

"Educated."

"Groomed."

"You have a very distrustful spirit, Ember."

"An actual benefit of the upbringing you'd claim to change."

"Enough of this circling around each other. You committed to this, remember?"

And what a fading devil's bargain that was turning out to be.

"Have you figured out the purpose of my sequoia?"

Ember held her breath and shook her head in answer. She had very few words she wanted to share with this deceitful Wizard. Not one of them was nice. Yet she had agreed to engage with him to learn as much as possible so she could stop reacting and start planning.

"Witches and Fae do not belong in Terra. I did my best to block the Convergence. Used every resource. It wasn't until we were trapped here that I discovered the cause and learned how to fix it."

"You told my mom this story." Ember narrowed her eyes. "That she could help send the mages back to their realms. And then you abandoned her."

"Yes. Regrettable, as I said before. However, there were tasks I had to complete outside this cursed bubble. All with the intention of setting things right. To. Fix. This." Tristan enunciated each word, his lips drawing thinner and his jaw muscles bulging, breaking his perfectly straight lines.

"This tree is the result of years of planning," he continued. "The seed was brought in from Heldu, our Witch realm. Souls were necessary for it to grow in a place where no magic resides. Its roots required access to the cave beneath us, where the energies of all three realms mingle. Only a few more things are needed."

"This will break the Veil."

"If the conditions are right," Tristan agreed. "Which is where you come in."

And they were back to the reason Ember started working with Tristan. She traded knowledge of her capabilities in exchange for training toward control. He taught her how to separate her power from herself, adding on the information about Charlah's soul within the tree as a supposed sign of good faith. A carrot that led her to this point; a promise that had drawn her own mother down a rabbit hole Susan couldn't crawl out of.

Ember shuffled backward. Working with Tristan left her afraid that some of the oil coating his words had contaminated her.

"Careful. You're very close to breaking a Fae rule."

With a glance over her shoulder, Ember's steps faltered. Inches away, the edge of the Fae border stretched in front of her, marked by vines clinging stubbornly to the trunks of redwoods. The plants, twisted and brittle in their winter state, curled like sleeping serpents, their heart-shaped leaves long gone with the change of season. In the warmer months, they would bloom—bright and vibrant against the bark—but here, in the stillness of No Man's Land, they seemed as lifeless as the ground beneath her feet.

The tree dominating the space had swallowed most of the clearing's expanse, leaving the borders tighter than Ember remembered. Shadows stretched between the branches, and the deadened forest floor cracked underfoot as she shifted away from the boundary. The cold air felt heavier the closer she got to the border, as if the land itself braced against the unnatural energy that pulsed beneath the towering trunk.

As Ember eased back, so not to disturb the fragile vines, her heart leapt at the sudden, solid pressure behind her. She spun, colliding with Tristan's chest, his presence silent as ever. His coat smelled faintly of pine and smoke, but his stillness held no warmth.

Fades! He must have used his magic to close the distance so fast. She took half a step back, caught between her father and the Fae.

Not a good place to be.

"Think about it, Ember. Not being limited to where you can walk anymore. Not being dictated to by the Fae. No longer required to check in with the Witches. Everyone returned to where they belong."

Ember swallowed the hope rising from her gut. This is what he'd promised her before, what had drawn her in. But she wasn't doing this for the mages, or even herself.

If the Fae and Witches left, then her mom would be free of magic. Susan wouldn't need the Halfers anymore. She could go back to being human. Her sacrifice seventeen years ago would be worth it. She could finally heal.

"If I said yes." Ember coughed out the hollow pain in her chest. "What would I have to do?"

Tristan stilled, breath bated as if intent on not breaking the moment. Ember mirrored his stillness.

"We will use your power to grow the sequoia—"

Ember eased back, Fae land or no. Her vision dimmed and her cheeks cooled with the loss of blood to her head. He wanted to feed her to the tree? Could she do that, even for Susan?

"Your power, not your soul." Tristan rushed to explain, his fingers gripping her arm through her red puff coat and pulling her around so he stood between her and the Fae. "The energy you create is pure. Concentrated and raw. That's what we've been practicing for, extending and then separating, just as you demonstrated by shielding your Halfer friend. Used in the correct way, your power can rip open this Veil bubble and reverse the Convergence. Mages will Fade into their own realms. Trifecta will belong to humans again."

Ember's mouth gaped. Any ability to hide thoughts or emotions had been swept away in the surge of Tristan's speech. Set everything right. Send everyone home. At the ambiguous price of working with Tristan. Trusting him.

Icy fear cut through her heated excitement.

Tristan was good, Ember had to admit. Was this how her mom had felt when he whispered his promises? What oily words wrapped in silk had he used on Susan?

"And what, let you lead me straight into pain?" She looked toward the tree, then jerked her arm away.

"There is pain either way."

The pair stood in silence as the shadows stretched and twisted with the slow rise of the morning sun. Pale light filtered through the towering redwoods, but it did little to chase away the lingering chill that clung to No Man's Land. The air felt thin, brittle, as if the forest itself held its breath.

Ember caught the faintest shift in Tristan's posture. He stood with a tautness to his stance—like a bowstring pulled back, waiting for the inevitable release. The silence between them wasn't empty; it hummed with unspoken words and warnings neither dared voice.

"I see you need to consider your options." Tristan granted her more space. "There is time for you to realize I'm correct. To understand that mages do not belong with humans and machines."

With Ember's next blink, Tristan was gone. Her eyes lingered on the impossible tree he left behind, its thick, unnatural form stretching skyward like a scar against the pale morning light. Her thoughts drifted, fragile and dangerous, bending toward things she knew better than to hope for.

A crunch of footsteps echoed through the forest, shattering the quiet. Ember spun to face the sound, shifting her weight, knees stiff from standing too long in the biting cold. Blood prickled in her legs as she shook them out, ready to run or fight—whichever the moment demanded.

Aaron Harwell emerged from the gaps between the redwoods, his figure distinct in the wash of sunlight filtering through the canopy. Ember inhaled slowly, steadying her breath as she squinted toward the sky. The sun had shifted higher. How long had she stood there? Had Chase already seen him?

Her gaze drifted back to Aaron. His familiar, easy steps grounded her, a stark contrast to the lingering chill that trailed after Tristan. The forest felt different now—less suffocating, but the weight of lost time pressed on her shoulders.

Thank goodness he hadn't shown up when she'd been talking to the Wizard.

It took Aaron a moment longer to spot Ember. The flat line of his mouth tilted into a lopsided grin and he broke into a jog. It was such a relief to see him over Tristan or Chase, or anyone else, that she fought against her own return smile.

"What are you doing here?" she snapped.

A frown flipped Aaron's lips, and he slowed his approach. Ember sighed and shook her head. She'd clearly overcompensated.

"Sorry. Are you okay? Chase said you were sick."

Aaron brightened. "So, you sound grumpy, but you're actually worried about me?"

She fought against it, she really did. Yet Aaron didn't miss the moment the warmth in her chest lightening the lines of her face.

"Are you ... Em, are you smiling?" Aaron's own grin doubled in size, as large and vibrant as the excitement that set his toes to bouncing.

"It's been known to happen," she assured him.

"Yes. In the depths of the forest where no human, Fae, or Witch eyes have ever seen."

Ember shook her head and puffed out an exasperated sigh. The light moment passed when Aaron's attention flickered toward the tree. He tried to refocus on her, but the imposing sequoia was impossible to ignore. Aaron took another ginger step forward, coming into No Mans' space for the first time.

"Chase said she's in there?"

"Yeah." Ember shifted between her feet, then moved to stand by his side.

"I realize we don't understand what this fading thing is supposed to be doing except that it's nothing good, but I hope Brandt is in there kicking her ass."

Ember flinched, tallying another reason to get the mages out of Trifecta.

"Yes, he was a dick. There's no excusing what he did to you. But. I mean. He didn't deserve—" Aaron sucked in a breath. "Sorry. This is hard to explain."

Good. The thought was sudden and harsh, a hot knife going through her chest.

An uncomfortable silence took over the space. Aaron rocked back on his heels, then rose onto his toes for a few nervous bounces.

"Hey. Thanks for asking how I was. I just wanted to look for myself." Aaron gestured toward the tree. "I'm on my way to see Chase."

"For coffee?" Ember meant to tease, but the words came out sharp. Aaron winced at the sound.

"It's … Are you coming?"

"No." Ember's reply was too quick. It piled onto the tension between them even though her answer had everything to do with her mother and nothing to do with him.

"I need to go see Devi," Ember surprised them both by saying. As spontaneous an excuse as it was, it made sense.

Devi Gerenne could give her a mage's perspective on Tristan's plan. Not that she'd tell the Witch everything.

"Oh. Tell her I'm sorry that she lost her mom. Except, no. Don't. She'd probably curse me for that, even miles away."

Ember forced a smile. "Probably."

"Okay. See you later?"

"Yeah." Her answer came out as a soft promise. An attempt to imply that though she was upset, she wasn't shutting him out.

Aaron nodded and then took off through the trees in his familiar, steady jog. Ember waited until he disappeared before she walked along the same path, hoping he didn't double back before she'd made it through the Halfer Zone and into The Circle.

Why was it so fading hard talking to him now that they were friends?

7

AARON

*A*aron hated leaving Ember behind like that. Her attitude stung. He didn't expect her to feel different, but wanted her to understand that being Brandt's friend hadn't been a bad thing. She might be willing to listen later, when they weren't both running on high emotions.

Aaron weaved between redwoods and brittle underbrush, heading for the spot where his street split from the main road. The pavement stretched uphill, winding past a row of run-down houses. Their cracked exteriors slumped in places, worn by time—or so it seemed. Beneath the rough edges, the Halfers had reinforced them, keeping the structures solid while the outside blended with Trifecta's forgotten corners.

Beyond the Halfer Zone, the pavement fractured and crumbled on Witch land. It didn't vanish—just shifted into something older and rougher, cutting through open ground with sparse trees lining the sides.

The opposite edge of Trifecta, called The End of the World, had once been Aaron's escape. If the road disappeared there, it would feel more fitting. Instead, it stretched on, a jagged path that wound down the mountainside. Human teens threw themselves at it religiously, Trifecta's version of coming of age. Yet no one broke through the silent, impassable verge-cursed barrier.

Lately, the Halfer houses pulled Aaron in more than the Edge. Aaron passed by a few mornings a week. What began as helping Chase gather rumors had turned into routine. The sharp bite of Halfer coffee stayed with him long after, anchoring him in ways he didn't entirely understand.

With a quiet curse, he realized he hadn't brought Chase's insulated tumbler with him. He'd been too intent on seeing the tree for himself, though he wasn't sure what closure he expected. Just because he'd experienced the consequences of magic didn't mean he understood it.

When he saw an unexpected person creeping between the houses in the Halfer Zone, he was suddenly very happy to not have the tumbler. It could be disastrous for Paul to catch him bringing that here, especially after his dad had made such a big deal about Aaron's secret friend.

Aaron abandoned his quest for Chase in an effort to derail Paul from whatever the human was trying to do. He caught up to his old soccer captain as he pounded with all his might against a boarded up door, one disguised to hide the fully functioning household behind it.

"Paul."

"What the—" Paul spun around, eyes wide and knitted cap falling to reveal his static-raised hair. "Verge, Aaron. What are you thinking, sneaking up on a guy like that?"

"What are you doing here? Dad sent you to see Janice."

Paul picked up his hat, glancing around as if suspecting someone might listen in, then he leaned toward Aaron.

"Kyle's here."

Aaron looked up at the neighborhood, eyes wide and heart pounding as he searched for Brandt's father. Kyle wasn't the most stable of guys, often drunk and with the tendency to become violent. Of course Paul would have stopped to check in, even taking Kyle home if he needed to.

"What's he doing?"

"Banging on doors." Paul waved up the street. "Trying to pry through boarded-up windows. Looking for signs of people staying here. Like that hasn't been done hundreds of times."

"He's looking for Brandt." Aaron blew out a heavy breath. Paul's lips pursed.

"Of course he's looking for his son. Do you really not care that your best friend is missing?"

Fury flooded Aaron, and he took a hard step toward Paul. His eyes burned as they focused on his old teammate, unblinking. He would not stand down while Paul suggested he wasn't concerned about where Brandt was. Especially when the truth was a lot harsher than their belief that Brandt disappeared to spend some cozy time with the other outcasts.

Paul took a step back, hands raised.

"Geeze, dude, lock it down. I apologize. That was a fading awful thing to say."

Aaron glared for another moment before taking a breath and backing off. He hadn't felt rage like that since Sophomore year, when he was trying to prove his soccer skills were legit and he wasn't on the team just because he was Coach's son.

"Yeah. Thanks. I'm sorry, too."

Paul gave a soft shake of his head and slapped Aaron's shoulder to show they were still good.

"There's nothing back here except a really fat raccoon."

A scratchy, but surprisingly sober voice echoed around the corner of a house a second before Kyle appeared. Brandt's father strode into sight, and Aaron stared at him a moment, struggling to recognizing him with combed hair and freshly shaved cheeks. Cleaned up, he looked a lot more like his son. Though his dark brown hair was peppered with silver, they shared the same strong cheekbones and light brown eyes.

"Mr. Miller," Aaron greeted quickly, widening his legs to stabilize his stance even as his thoughts swirled into chaos. "How are you?"

"Better in some ways. Worse in others. Losing a son helps with perspective." He studied Aaron, his features tightening and relaxing as if he fought with a few competing emotions. "How about you, kid? I know you and Brandt—"

Aaron interrupted by clearing his throat. "Yeah. I kinda expected him to crawl out of hiding by now."

At a different time, that would have been true. Brandt's pattern was to disappear when problems with Kyle escalated or overwhelming life challenges surfaced. Part of Aaron wished he was still clueless, but more of him appreciated knowing what oppositions Trifecta faced, and having new friends he trusted to tackle them.

Ignorance might be bliss, but it was more limiting than being stuck in Trifecta.

"I suppose you've already knocked on all these doors?" Kyle asked.

"Ah." Aaron reclaimed his hand and used it to comb through his curls. Let the guys guess that meant 'yes' rather than, 'yeah, but only the one I knew would open.'

"Did, um, something tip you off? That the runaways might live here?" Aaron peered around Paul and Kyle as if trying to see between the carefully placed boards on the windows.

"Honestly? This isn't the first place I wanted to look," Kyle said.

"But it was closest," Paul answered quickly, clearly knowing the direction of Kyle's thoughts.

"Where were you wanting to search?" Aaron asked, ignoring Paul's scowl and tense shake of his head.

"Brandt." Kyle swallowed, closing his eyes for a moment, then opening them with new conviction. "I can't remember it all. He came at night, I think. I lost track of time, but maybe a few weeks ago? He said that the Trimarked bitch had thrown him out. He was going to take care of her with a special knife."

Aaron froze. Paul thinned his lips, eyes narrowed, silently berating Aaron for making the mistake of asking.

"The Trimarked girl isn't missing," Paul spoke calmly.

"But she could know where he is!" Kyle shouted, his voice echoing up the road, bouncing between the houses and trees.

"I already asked her."

Kyle and Paul paused, looking at Aaron as if he'd admitted to knowing where Brandt was all along. Aaron flinched, shoving his hands into his hip pockets and cursing his slip. How was he supposed to explain without going into details or appearing more guilty?

"I've been desperate, too," he stumbled. "I asked the Trimarked girl, and I even visited the Witches. All I got from them was a weird flower lesson." Along with a spell that apparently helped him run through the forest while suffering from a stab wound, but Aaron kept that part to himself.

"You are a good friend," Kyle rasped. "But she could be lying. She has to be lying. If I found her and just talked to her, tell her Brandt is my son —"

Aaron swallowed.

Was this what Gus had been trying to warn him about when he'd referred to Ember earlier? Had Kyle already spoken with Gus about this, but hadn't been believed? Few would accept Kyle Miller at his word, but Aaron knew this story must be true, even if Kyle's memory was faulty.

Aaron's stomach twisted. He looked down the street toward Town, thrusting his fingers into his hair and gripping the curls.

He had to forget about warning Chase right now. His immediate concern was finding a way to satisfy Kyle and Paul, to keep up appearances while wearing them out on their search. Given their states of mind, he couldn't let these two humans get caught up with the mages or Ember.

The last time one of his friends had gone up against the Trimarked Child, they'd ended up dead. Not that it was Ember's fault, but it was a truth Aaron couldn't forget.

"So what's next on your list?" Aaron asked. "You said you wanted to search a few places?"

"I thought about the Trimarked girl's house first, but it's been destroyed." Kyle took a deep breath, leaning in now that he felt listened to. "The front door was ripped off, animals have moved in. So they have to be somewhere else. If not here, then there's the forest between Fae and humans. That makes the most sense."

"That's … a lot of ground to cover." Aaron sighed. "So I suppose we get started?"

Kyle practically glowed when Aaron agreed to help, which only caused guilt to gnaw a little more heavily in his gut. But exploring the empty forest while Ember met with Devi seemed both safe and the perfect way to exhaust Kyle. Paul still looked to be in good shape, but he didn't seem as eager to engage in this search.

"Did you want to head to Town?" Aaron asked his friend. "Finish that errand with Janice?"

"No, I'm not going to leave you alone with—" Paul cut off, his eyes flickering to Kyle. "When you might run into trouble."

"Dad said he wanted it done before people get out of work."

"Hopefully, this won't take that much time." Paul's pointed glance showed he thought the same as Aaron. Kyle might have cleaned up, but his fitness must be poor given his before-today lifestyle. He shouldn't last long.

"Yeah," Aaron agreed, working to hide his disappointment.

"This is great." Kyle clapped his palms and rubbed them together, his cheeks flushed with renewed energy. "I'm sure we'll find something. And when we reach the barrier, we can look for holes."

"Holes?" Aaron asked.

"Right." Paul turned slightly, so only Aaron saw him roll his eyes. "Because if the bitch did throw Brandt out, then the evidence might still be there."

"Exactly." Kyle nodded with enough force to knock his combed hair out of place.

"O-okay."

Kyle strode down the road, ready to get going. Paul gripped Aaron's arm and scowled.

"What are you doing, encouraging him? The man is heartbroken and sick."

"Same as you, I guess, knocking on these doors," Aaron shot back, then gave a shrug. "Come on. Let's wear him out, then take him home. Then we'll find my dad and he can handle Kyle."

Paul's shoulders dropped and he let out a forceful breath before jogging to catch up with their old teammate's father. Aaron glanced along the houses, ensuring that nothing was disturbed, then walked quickly after the duo he'd reluctantly made a trio.

8

EMBER

The Circle was distinctly quiet that morning as Ember stepped from the gravel road to the meticulously cut stone pavers set by the Witches. She picked her steps with care, the heavy air a warning not to disturb the tenuous balance of the space.

Witches generally rose with the sun. By the time Ember usually made her way in, they were already working with the soil, healing the earth, tearing apart the concrete and separating out subnatural elements left over from the days this area contained a thriving glass-making plant and bottled water factory.

With Leona gone, they had other things to heal.

Ember hoped Devi was in her usual space as she made her way past the curated paths. She wound through flower beds that thrived despite the frigid temperatures of November. The carved stone fountain stood tall and quiet, the magic that pulled the water from its underground source at rest. A shiver tickled along Ember's spine at the emptiness. Once, she would have preferred sneaking in to meet Devi without dozens of gemstone eyes watching her every move.

Not like this, though. Not because of grief.

She passed the vine-encrusted factory-turned-apartment building, and most of the Witch improvements stopped just past it. The concrete world of humans had been torn apart. Neat but awkward piles of rubble were scattered in what used to be driveways and parking spaces. The right-hand path led to more developments, but Ember's destination took her deeper into the mess.

A long storage warehouse appeared on her left, lined with multiple bays marked by rolling gates closed against the cold while they waited for semi-trucks that weren't coming. This time, Ember's steps slowed for a different reason. Only a few days ago, she'd made this trip with a perilous purpose. They'd been trying to save the Coven from the deranged Witch Queen. They'd had to take shelter in a garage further up the line.

Ember chewed her lip, her eyes on the fourth bay where Devi worked. Would the Witch return after the confrontation with Charlah? One of the last places she'd seen her mother alive?

Only one way to find out.

Usually, the large gate was open, tucked against the ceiling. Today it was closed, so Ember reached for the access door. She paused, wondering for the first time if it was wise to disturb Devi without an invitation. Clearing her throat, Ember committed to turning the handle. She pushed the door open only enough to squeeze through, closing it immediately. Doing her best not to recreate that moment three days ago where the enemy had arrived silhouetted by backlight.

Ember waited until her eyes adjusted to the gloom. This garage was different from the one where they'd confronted Charlah. It didn't have large machinery stored along the sides, but had barrels of some kind of oil waste that Devi had been experimenting with. Across the room, Ember sighed with relief to recognize the cranberry hair shining under a single bank of lights. The Witch bent over a notebook, writing furiously with her left hand while holding something small in her right.

"Devi," Ember called gently, stepping forward as tentatively as she'd done in the outside quiet. Devi hummed, a sign she was listening even though it didn't look like it. Ember stopped across from the Witch, noting the circular sketch on the working page and how it matched the matte black ring pinched between Devi's fingers.

"Do me a favor and take this. Like you did a few days ago."

Ember recoiled. "It nearly blew me up last time."

"I have a theory. Try it."

Ember activated her power, forming a shield across her skin as its energetic barrier had been the only way to get close to the ring before. As she reached forward, the dragon bone circlet vibrated within Devi's grip, blurring with the tension. With Ember still centimeters away, the piece of Fae-made jewelry disappeared into its own reverberations. When Devi lifted her writing hand, the black band appeared on her middle finger, as if it had been there the whole time.

Devi's lips tilted up in a self-satisfied smile. She placed her pencil on her notebook and gave Ember her full, if reluctant, attention.

"No."

"I didn't even say anything."

"It doesn't matter. That's my answer. I'm so tired of people asking me to do things. To take on my mother's mantle, as if the Coven passed the title of High Priestess from parent to child. Which they don't, by the way. They just want me to be her. To pretend to be her. All I want is to be here."

The words spilled out of Devi's trembling lips. Her mint-green eyes sparkled in their gem-like depths, bearing a fiery torment Ember could only vaguely understand.

"I'm sorry."

"So is everyone else."

Ember took a deep breath. Devi's emotions were high, a

reaction Ember was used to seeing but only in regard to her projects. This ran deeper. Her ring experiment was clearly a cover, a task meant to keep her mind busy so she wouldn't have to feel.

Ember could help her with that.

"Devi, does the Coven want to return to Heldu?"

"What kind of question is that? Of course they do."

"How badly? Would they be willing to work with someone they don't trust?"

Devi narrowed her eyes, their pain-filled backlight fading as her analytical brain took over.

"Your powers have been growing. Did you discover something? Or are you coming to confess?"

Devi thought Ember was talking about herself, not Tristan. Perhaps that was a deception she could run with, though, given Devi's current state.

"Not anything new. Just a theory."

Devi lifted a finger and tapped her pursed lips. Ember locked her fists against her thighs, stopping her fingers from tapping against the fabric of her jeans.

"You're acting weird," Devi charged.

"Aren't we all after what happened?"

"Hmm."

Devi didn't sound convinced, but her eyes drifted to her notes, then to the ring on her finger. Her grip closed around it.

"Maybe," Devi agreed. "But to practice. Ember, the Fae are still the Fae. It isn't a good idea. And the last time you wrestled with the barrier, Nicu threw his tattoos off his body to reach you."

"What?"

Ember's voice was sharp, her breath scarce. With wide eyes she studied Devi, who replied with a casual shrug, "It's not an ordinary Fae skill. I wouldn't bet on him being able to do it again."

Ember shook her head, clearing out the new information to

focus on her goal. Devi's dismissal of Ember's idea suggested the Witches had boundaries they wouldn't cross, even if it meant going home. It seemed Tristan was working more alone than Ember thought. Or did he have secret allies within The Circle? If there were, would Devi know?

"And you think that's true? For everyone in the Coven?"

Devi tossed her pencil on the table and leaned back in her chair, arms crossed.

"You want honesty? It's likely. There are thousands of us, and everyone is susceptible to temptation. I'm sure a few of them have considered kidnapping you and examining how your power might work. To see if we can tap into it and use it to our benefit. But temptation doesn't lead directly to action. The Coven acts in Trifecta's best interests, securing our place in it. For now, our efforts need to be focused on finding the Queen. Besides, Mom would never allow the Coven to harm you."

Devi flinched as she caught up to her own words, then shook her head and leaned forward, hands clasped over the table.

Ember swallowed against her aching throat, dropping a nod. Sometimes Devi's objective perspective forgot there was a person on the other end of it. She wasn't surprised to learn there were Witches who thought about capturing her, but Devi's use of the word 'we' had cut deeper than expected.

"Do you know the legend of the Ternate?" Devi asked.

The abrupt change of subject startled Ember, giving her a way out of the spiral of her darker thoughts.

"What?"

"The Chaos Star. Do you know about it?"

"Should I?"

"Nicu may have told you. It's tied to all of this somehow. The star cluster isn't typical, as it doesn't have a regular orbit. When it rises, big changes happen. For example, it appeared for a single day when you were born. It rose again the night Brandt was thrown out of Trifecta and hasn't set since."

Pressure built behind Ember's forehead. Devi's scattered thoughts and knowledge bombs had left her emotionally bruised.

Maybe coming here had been a mistake. Ember had always seen Devi as impassive, objective, and separate. Yet there she sat, dark bags beneath her eyes, cheeks a little more hollow. Ember debated asking Devi how she was, but then she remembered Chase's insistence that they focus on anything else, just so he could keep it together.

"I should go."

"Be careful." Devi's last warning followed Ember, soothing some of the hurt the Witch's comments caused. In the space between, a detail floated up, stopping Ember in her tracks.

"You should know that Charlah is gone. Tell the Coven, too."

"What are you talking about?"

Devi's words shot out in a burst so hot they would have caught on fire if magic had been involved.

"The tree got her."

Devi flushed, then paled, her palms pressing flat against the table. Her lips trembled.

"See you," Ember said into the quiet, not knowing what else to say. Not knowing if she should have said anything. She slipped from the cavernous unloading bay in the same quick way she'd entered.

As Ember walked, her fingertips tapped a steady rhythm on her thighs. The Circle remained empty, the air still hollow. With each step, she sunk deeper into thoughts so complex they didn't have words. Shifting from one impression to the next, images fluttered past and burst apart.

Whether or not there were Coven members working with Tristan, Devi's offhanded acceptance that there were likely Witches and Wizards willing to capture Ember set her nerves on edge. What if Leona had truly been the only one holding them back? What if her casual visits to The Circle weren't safe anymore?

Ember picked up her pace and crossed quickly into human territory.

"Stay away from the magic," her mom had said.

"Don't let them see you," Nicu demanded.

Two warnings Ember hadn't taken seriously until it was too late.

Then today, from two separate people: *Be careful.*

Blue light flickered against Ember's hands and she drew her shaking fists to her chest, worried this last piece of advice would be another she'd fail to follow.

A door creaked open, breaking through the winter quiet. Ember spun around to face it, burying her hands in her coat pockets to hide the sparks between her fingers even as she struggled to get them under control.

Chase stepped out of the smallest house at the end of the street, the one that held the Halfers' stores and led to the secret mirrored entrance to the Club. His focus was downward, as if his frown was too heavy to hold.

A deep breath shuddered through her and the sparks faded away as relief surged. Ember continued along the road and Chase's attention jerked toward her, the thoughtful scowl turning into confusion.

"You saw the Witches?" he asked on approach.

"I checked in with Devi." A simple enough answer. She couldn't share the whole truth, and wasn't ready to discuss the painful bits.

Chase shifted his focus to where the pavement crumbled into gravel and led toward The Circle.

"How is she?"

"Sharp. Angry. Focused on a new puzzle."

"Good. We need our distractions right now."

"You're distracting yourself?"

"Yeah." Chase cleared his throat, blinking rapidly. "Let's not talk about that part."

"Okay." Ember tapped her fingers against her jacket as she watched Chase press his hands into the long pockets of his coat.

"Did you see Aaron?" As she'd hoped, the question brought a softness to Chase's features and his shoulders dropped into a more relaxed position. Ember questioned the human's calming effect on the Halfer, but then, Aaron tended to break through people's walls as if they hadn't been built to last. Including her own.

"Yeah. We didn't chat for long, but I had time to update him. He feels better now that he knows. Speaking of..." Chase watched Ember out of the corner of his eye, as if he wasn't willing to fully face her. "I shared the news about the Queen with the Halfers, too. They know they can return to their homes, but most of them are choosing to stay at the Club."

"They don't trust me."

Chase shrugged. "It doesn't really matter. They don't feel safe and that's that. In fact, there are six who want out."

Now it made sense why he didn't meet her eyes directly.

"What's the schedule? We aren't due to send supplies for a few days, but even then, if it's one at a time —"

"They want to leave immediately. All together."

"W-what?" Ember tucked her gloved hands under her arms.

"I know," Chase murmured. "But look, they're panicked. Too scared to think straight. I got them to calm down by promising to ask."

"Ask?"

"If you think you can do six. I mean, you did that thing with me and the shield, so maybe you're getting stronger?"

"You want this too," Ember realized. Chase finally met her gaze head on.

"You want to know why your skills have been so important? How you've more than pulled your weight? Having disgruntled Halfers around isn't ideal, not with as many secrets as we're juggling. So you give them an out. I provide them with a job, keeping an eye out for anything unexpected, or a chance to leave the mountain completely. No matter what, it keeps them from going to the mages or the humans."

"Oh. And the exit spot?"

Chase coughed. "We need to send them out close to the camp. That's near The End of the World so they can watch the road. It's right around where you threw Brandt out."

Though the land was human, that area was part of the Fae's hunting grounds, which meant that getting caught was a real threat. Ember pushed out a forceful breath, looking toward the sun. She'd been out for hours already and though it was lunch time, she wasn't hungry.

What Chase asked of her was terribly risky. When they usually let people out, they chose a spot deep into human land, keeping as far from the mages as possible. Letting out one person was a matter of a few seconds. Letting out more would be that compounded since there had to be space between the bodies, plus added width because of packs filled with provisions and supplies to support them on the outside.

Six Halfers would take at least a minute to pass through, which mattered when your task was secret and dangerous. With Tristan's lessons and her own practice, not to mention the power surge she'd just clamped down on, it was likely she could hold the barrier for that long. But those additional bodies making noise and all that extra time increased their chances of getting caught.

Yet she owed Chase. Even more now that he'd taken Susan in. Both Ember and her mother were staying in his own private house. Not to mention, letting these Halfers out would increase their security, according to Chase. Peace of mind was a gift they could all use.

"Yeah," she agreed with a misty puff of breath. "Let's do it. We just have to be careful."

Ember winced at her own words. Every choice she made lately seemed more and more poised to tempt fate.

Whatever Chase thought about her reaction, he kept it to himself. He nodded as his eyes gained a faraway look she'd come to recognize as his 'making plans' expression.

"Great. I'll gather them up, then. They're probably already packed. When can you be ready?"

"Now. I mean, once they are. Let's get this over with."

9

DEVI

evi heaved in a deep, shaky breath as soon as Ember closed the door.

Charlah was gone.

She wanted to be happy, to accept the poetic justice found in the fact that the damn soul-sequoia had eaten her. Instead, it felt as if the power had been snatched from one of her spells. She hadn't made concrete plans to pursue the Queen, but she'd held tight to the knowledge that she would.

Charlah had murdered her mom, and the tree stole her revenge.

Squeezing her eyes shut, fingernails cutting into her palms, Devi opened her mouth to a throat-ravaging scream that left her ears ringing in the silence behind the echo.

She dropped her head, scratching at her scalp as she knotted cranberry tresses between her fingers, struggling to hold on to anything concrete.

It had been all she could do to feign interest in Ember's conversation. Trying to focus. Jumping topics. Finding random things to say to project the image of being at least a little okay. At one point, Devi almost lost it when Ember's eyes went soft, dreading the moment she was asked how she was.

But by some welcome blessing, Ember had kept the question to herself. If she'd inquired, it would have been impossible for Devi to imitate normalcy.

But then the news of Charlah's demise broke through Devi's fog with a hammer.

Before Ember's visit, Devi hadn't even known what time it was, as she'd been awake for an untold number of hours. She had no interest in dreams filled with scattered images of those last moments in the cave. Whenever she fled them, sleep led her to visions of an angry Wizard and dozing dragons. A diviner might help her, but approaching the Coven would result in being dragged in to perform a duty she wasn't qualified for and felt a savage resistance toward.

As if Devi had the capacity to care how the Coven functioned. She wouldn't even inherit the High Priestess role. They wanted her to stand in while they figured out who to vote for, expecting her to pretend to have her mother's peace-keeping ability and fill in doing whatever Leona had done each and every day. But Devi did not possess those capabilities or expertise.

The warehouse had been Devi's life. It was here where she spent most of her hours figuring out how to conduct her investigations without Leona knowing her true goals or the inherent danger her experiments presented. As a result, she'd devoted so little time to her mom…

Devi choked on the pressure in her chest and coughed out a strangled sob. Her cheeks burned with the onslaught of fresh heartache, her skin already raw and dry from the stain of salt and sorrow. She pressed her forehead into the table against the assault, arms wrapped tightly around her head to keep from falling apart like an unraveled spell.

Eventually, the tears stopped. Devi patted her sore cheeks with the sleeves of her russet sweater, then rested her chin on crossed forearms. Without the energy to hold up her eyelashes, she let them drop, allowing the weight of her body to compress under a grief greater than gravity. Cool air filled her nose and painted her overheated brain, but there was no methodology to circumvent or pause her breakdown. She could only exist within it.

Something scraped against the concrete, generating a sound that didn't belong. Devi opened her eyes, seeing the disturbed dust motes floating in the air. Had an animal found its way into the building, seeking shelter from the November cold? Her gaze scanned the floor, looking for the twitching nose of a rat or the striped tail of a raccoon.

The foot she discovered was reptilian and as large as a bull-frog, with long, curved claws. Blue-green scales blended well with the gloom of the warehouse bay. A rounded, narrow snout rested low to the ground, supported by a short, thick neck decorated with toothy spines that continued along its barrel torso and a tapered tail.

"A dragonling." Devi whispered the words, her voice as broken as her heart. Had she fallen asleep after all? But no. Intense anguish still tied her limbs, and she wasn't fighting images from the cave. This part was real. She expected her natural curiosity to rise, or a spike of fear, but neither happened. Maybe she could pretend, though, and fake her way back to normal.

"What are you doing on Terra?"

The creature tiptoed forward, pressing under the table. Devi waited for it to reappear. When it didn't, an unexpected burst of panic burned away at her frozen limbs. She pushed her chair back and peeked beneath, relieved to find its rounded snout nearly at her knees, as if it were the exact friend she needed right now.

But why? Her brow furrowed against the heat behind her eyes as her mind struggled to function. Had she met this dragon before? At first glance, the prospect seemed impossible, yet Devi's instincts wouldn't allow her to dismiss the idea that easily.

The dragons in her dreams were full-grown, off in the distance. She would appear on a grassy field next to a deep lake, she and the giant lizards happy to avoid each other. She'd never seen a dragonling there, and only recognized it from books that referenced the Fae and their realm of Gypsum, the only dimension where dragons lived.

Devi extended her left hand to test if the creature would approach. It pressed its dry nose against her palm, the eyelids shifting until they had a gentle curve reminiscent of a smile. She released a shuddering breath with the simple touch, confirmation this wasn't a dream. Contact that didn't expect anything from her. The dragonling's scales held an unexpected warmth and the knots in Devi's shoulders and back unwound as the heat drifted from their point of connection and into her body.

She slipped from the chair to the floor, drawn in by the promise of kindness and unconditional comfort. The dragonling let out a tranquil sigh. Its eyes closed, its head resting heavily in her lap, as if it had waited for contact with her for years instead of minutes.

The heaviness in Devi's mind shifted and eased its pressure from around her heart. The heavy weight of loss still lived there, sharp-edged and dangerous. But now it settled into the background and allowed a tickle of curiosity. The sensation grew and drew Devi's attention to the ring.

It was a smooth, matte piece of jewelry. It held no writing or other markings, but from what Devi recalled, dragon bone was one of the hardest materials in all of existence. That the Fae had crafted it into a circular band was miraculous. The lore claimed the artifact protected against the dragon hive mind, which was why her mother had thought it might help break the Queen's connective magic.

"Are you tied to this? Is this how you found me?"

The dragonling shifted its head, breathing hot air onto her hand, its right eye peeking open. Devi caught the glint of its iris, and the vibrancy of color reverberated within Devi's brain, igniting connections in a burst of understanding.

Rainbow-colored eyes met her own. More than that, she recognized them. She'd been two years old at the time, and already a phenomenon. Where most children her age were learning to put together sentences, Devi was developmentally closer to four. It happened with some mages; few enough to be unexpected, but common enough that they were prepared.

"Why were you in our archives?" Devi whispered the question, not expecting an answer. The dragonling widened its prismatic eye, its nose easing toward her hand until the soft scales brushed against the dragon bone artifact. The contact opened a connection into her mind, pulling forth a memory nearly eighteen years old.

}|{

"You can look, but don't touch." Leona watched as little Devi folded her hands together behind her back to show her mom she understood. They didn't usually allow two-year-olds in here, but the High Priestess was her mommy, and Devi was super smart and really big. The healer said she wasn't the only little girl to grow up so fast, but everyone who did turned out really special. So special that Leona let Devi come into the archives with her, but only if she followed the rules.

Leona's mass of carrot-red curls bounced against her face when she nodded. Devi liked to watch her mom's hair dance, and sometimes she'd use magic to make it fly around. Leona had laughed at first, but then Devi had done it too often and she'd been forced to stop. She didn't want to lose the archives, too, so each and every rule would be followed perfectly.

The archives was a special room in the basement of the factory the Witches had made into apartments. It was the only improved building so far. As the Coven prepared to break up the black ground and reveal pure earth, Leona searched through the artifacts for something that would help return the hard stuff into a natural state.

Devi took careful steps into the room. Her slower pace meant Leona left her sightline, but that part was okay. Devi liked to walk by herself, taking the path on the outside. The aisles alternated with back-to-back shelving first, then lines of tables next, the furniture scavenged from where the humans used to work.

Shelves in one row were beautifully decorated with large natural stones, crafted items in another. Stone and metal bowls of various sizes covered the table tops closer to the door, then weapons appeared further in with different swords, sheathes, and long, gnarled staffs. Devi paused at one of her favorite artifacts, the piece of twisted glass Leona said was created by lightning striking sand.

After ten rows, Devi reached the end of the space. She walked up the last aisle between a table set and a wall covered in portraits, mirrors, and intricate reliefs made of wood, stone, and clay. Nicknamed the gallery, Devi loved this part because she was big enough to see most of the stuff.

A clattering pulled her attention to the corner as she approached. Was her mom there? Devi eased in, not wanting to startle her in case she held that dark thing that sucked in all light and color and could only be touched with gloves. Devi shuffled to a stop when she saw something other than her mother. A lizard stood in front of her, so big that they were the same height, though the creature was a lot longer. It stared at her with its head turned, one large, rainbow eye studying her.

They had a dragonling in the archives? Like from her story books? Devi's heartbeat quickened in her small chest, her eyes expanding as she tried to take it all in.

"Who are you? I haven't seen you before."

Leona said that as long as she didn't touch anything, she was safe. If she followed the same rule here, she would be fine. Devi crept closer, excited when the animal didn't run away. On her next step, though, the lizard took two steps, then paused while keeping its bright rainbow eye on her, as if it wanted her to follow.

Devi looked around for her mom, scared that she might be doing something wrong by playing with the dragonling. But the creature made a gesture with its head, just like a person guiding her. A grin split Devi's face as bubbles of excitement sprung through her and she covered her mouth to block the sound of her squeal. The next time the lizard came close, it put its snout tenderly against her skirt, grabbing it between gentle teeth and tugging with extreme care.

It did want to play!

Just don't touch it back and mom won't get mad.

The dragonling eased backward, a low, purr-like chirp expanding its neck. Devi followed it into the corner, where it tucked itself under a table and encouraged her to follow. Did it want to play hide and seek?

Devi paused, trying to snatch back her skirt. Hiding was definitely against the rules. She should call out to her mom, but her tongue stuck to the roof of her mouth. The dragonling tugged again just as Devi heard the heavy, crisp footsteps of a person she wanted to avoid. Losing all hesitation, Devi ducked and scrambled into place.

Though there wasn't a tablecloth to shield them, this table had long, flexible pieces of ribbon pouring over the edges. The Coven used them in springtime for the Maypole. For now, they were all draped along the table, and separated like a rainbow. The parts hanging over the edge were thick enough that she and the dragonling shouldn't be noticed if they stayed really, really still.

Devi was happy to hide. The steady thumps were not her mother's soft, almost dancing steps. They belonged to the one Wizard in Trifecta who scared her. Every movement he made was stiff, and when others weren't looking, his emerald eyes always narrowed like he was mad at everything.

The Wizard walked along the last row of metal shelves and stopped about midway. He paused as if listening for something, then reached up to the top shelf and took down a narrow box of dark wood. Flipping it open, he wasted no time removing a bright, silvery knife from its container and slipping it into an inner pocket of his long coat.

He stole it! Devi pressed both hands over her mouth, her breath hot against the tops of her fingers as she watched him walk away. She turned to the dragonling, but the creature had disappeared. She searched wildly for it, or for the Wizard, but she was alone.

"Mama!"

Devi scrambled out from under the table, sprinting up the outer aisle, watching for her mother between the shelves. Leona stepped out from one near the front. She wore her soft expression that usually calmed Devi down right away, but this time it wasn't enough.

Leona knelt, a hand behind her back, and that pretty smile melted into a frown. She brushed a cobweb from Devi's bright curls, her amethyst eyes flicking over her daughter as if she could determine what was wrong by looking at her outsides.

"Tristan stole a knife." Devi pointed toward the back of the archive.

"Did he see you?"

"No. The dragonling hid me."

"What? There is no dragonling in here, Devi. Are you sure you saw Tristan?"

"Yes! He took a shiny knife from the black box."

Leona whispered a naughty word and Devi curled her lips in between her teeth, rocking back. Her mom stood up to retrace her steps down the aisle to where she'd left a small container open on the table. She dropped the artifact she'd held behind her back, but it didn't fall straight like normal things. Instead, it arced through the air, heading toward Devi.

"No!" Leona shouted, catching the ring in mid flight. She sucked in a deep breath, eyes wide on her daughter.

"Where did you see this dragonling?" Leona's voice sounded weird, as if she was talking with food in her mouth, which was against the rules.

"In the back. Where Tristan took the knife."

"Right." Leona pushed the ring into the box, closing the lid so it pressed against her fingers. The circlet rattled against the wood even as Leona snapped it shut, flipping the latch and wrapping it with a length of hemp twine to make sure it stayed closed. She turned to the shelves behind her and rose up on her toes to place the artifact as high as possible before refocusing on Devi.

"Let's go see what Tristan took, hmm? Can you show me?"

"Yes!" Devi agreed, happy to be a helper to her mom, who was the absolute best Witch Devi knew and would make Tristan return whatever he stole.

}I{

Devi's thoughts slowly returned to the present. She absently petted the dragonling with her right hand while the left fidgeted with the black ring.

Interesting that the day Tristan took the knife was the same day she'd met the lizard and seen the dragon bone ring for the first time. As a set of three, the omens were impossible to ignore. Another thought tickled at the edges, remembering that in each instance Tristan used the starfall blade to cut through Trifecta's barrier, the Ternate had rested above the horizon.

There it was. A mystery worth exploring. A deliciously complex puzzle with enough missing pieces to keep Devi's brain occupied and away from the thoughts that had kept her stuck in this room.

"Now I just need a quiet place to study where there won't be any interruptions. I'd use my cave, but..." Devi's mouth twisted with the weight of grief that had baked itself into her soul. Even if the cavern hadn't been where her mother was killed, she couldn't return when it was filled with the roots of a tree that devoured souls.

The dragonling shifted, gripping a ruffle of her sapphire skirt and giving a gentle tug, just as it had eighteen years ago.

"You know a spot?"

Another tug appeared to be an affirmative answer, then the dragonling released her. Devi stood, brushing off her clothes and looking over her stacks of notebooks and cups of pencils. "Let me grab a few things. Then we can go."

10

EMBER

*E*mber walked with Chase as they led the six Halfers who wanted out through the forest. They'd skirted between the last of the human homes and No Man's, no one wanting the memory of the tree, even if it did show signs that Charlah was no longer a threat.

A Halfer elbowed his way between Chase and Ember.

"You're sure she can do this?"

"Relax, Seth." Chase peeked around the rude Halfer to check on Ember. She sidestepped to put more space between them. His little shove was reminiscent of the hair pulls and tugs the Halfers had exposed her to since she'd been living with them. At least she wouldn't have to endure him for much longer.

Seth kept himself between the Halfer leader and Ember, his lips thinning as he continued to watch her.

"Rumor has it that you can't go onto Fae land. So why are we walking so close?"

"It's temporary."

Ember glanced up to see the naked vines strung along branches about ten feet from the ground that worked as an unofficial border marker. In a few more yards, they'd take a

78

path leading toward the exit point, leaving the Fae's territory behind.

"How do you know—"

Chase's question turned into a shout when Seth deviated his stride as they entered a gap between the trees, shoving Ember with his shoulder. She stumbled across the uneven forest floor. Panic cleared every thought from her mind, cold air stuck in her lungs. She threw her arms out, her right hand crossing that forbidden border, her fingers fading into mist.

What?

Ember twisted, pulling her arm to her chest as she forced a fall onto her left shoulder. She used the momentum to roll herself away from the barrier, eyes closed against the concentrated burn she felt at the ends of her forefingers.

"Ember!" Chase was at her side, helping her sit up. "Are you okay? Seth, you fading gull!"

Seth spat at the use of the slang word meant as an insult to humans. "You're showing preference for your precious mutant."

"I'm showing a lack of preference for your lack of intelligence," Chase countered. "Did you even take a moment to think that the Fae probably have a magical means to let them know when they have trespassers? That they'd absolutely know if the Trimarked passes through? If they don't catch onto us, you're out first."

Seth paled, though he lifted his chin in continued defiance. "Good," he spat, as if that had been his plan all along. Chase pointed him toward their path, dismissing him as he gripped the wrist of the fist Ember cradled to her chest.

"What happened?" Chase asked.

"I'm not sure." She exposed her aching digits, expecting them to be raw or charred. Yet, they looked perfectly fine, though her fingernails were half an inch long. She stared, wide-eyed, lifting her left hand for comparison, showing nails trimmed short and neat. Chase frowned, taking both her hands in his and running a thumb over her nail beds.

"They weren't this uneven before?"

Ember shook her head, stunned at the difference in her aching fingers.

"It was only a second."

"Who knows what magic Fae put into that border?" Chase offered.

"Do you think they know?"

Chase's green eyes flashed to Ember's silver, and he stood with an abrupt inhale, glaring at the offending Halfer.

"If they do, they'll be on us soon, so let's hurry. I don't want Seth to miss his chance to fall off."

"You think the Fae will come?" Seth's skin paled, and he looked deeper into Fae territory.

"The way they keep tabs on her?" Chase snapped. "Yeah."

Another Halfer grabbed Seth by his forearm and force marched him forward, tearing him from Ember and Chase while getting them closer to their goal. They whispered in fierce bursts, a quiet argument suggesting they might have planned this together, but hadn't considered the consequences beyond taking one last shot at the Trimarked Girl.

Chase helped Ember stand up. She brushed forest debris from her coat and jeans, pulling pine needles from where they poked through her hair. As she worked, the burning sensation in her right hand eased, leaving a low tingle in its wake. Chase remained next to her after that, trailing the other Halfers instead of leading them, as if he wanted to keep an eye on them.

Each minute of the rest of the walk strained against dense anticipation. Ember focused her hearing, even though there was no way they'd detect the Fae's approach. All mages walked in near silence, and she was in a group of eight humans who crunched through and trampled the dry undergrowth of the forest. When the shimmering power of the dome finally echoed within Ember's bones, she rolled out the ache in her shoulders.

"Stop," she called, knowing she was the only one who could sense it. Making her way to the front, Ember approached the invisible shield with a mix of trepidation and respect. The Veil encompassing the city of Trifecta hadn't always been nice to her. Would it be today?

Not a constructive consideration when speed was required.

"When will she —"

"It's a process," Chase cut off Seth's question. "Which wouldn't be a problem if we weren't worrying about pixies materializing, would it?"

Seth scowled, but retreated in the face of Chase's accusation. Ember rolled her shoulders, trying to appreciate the extra space. For the past month, Ember had needed a few minutes to get beyond the memory of this power swallowing her whole.

"Nicu threw his tattoos off his body to reach you," Devi had said. *"I wouldn't bet on him being able to do it again."*

After her brush with the Fae border, would he even want to? Would he pause as he'd done before to gauge her intent? Or was contact with Fae energy that line he wouldn't forgive her for crossing?

She had to move. To get out of here. Maybe hide underground, even if that meant watching Susan play house with kids who weren't hers. And for that, Ember needed to open this barrier and expel the fading Halfers.

One last deep breath. Ember raised her right hand, fingertips trembling as she ignored the unnatural growth of her nails. Though contact was necessary, this time she wouldn't tap out the pattern she'd believed had been why the barrier opened for her. In her lessons with Tristan, she'd learned the truth about the Veil, and how her power communicated with it. Control came from enforcing her will.

An arch rippled into existence. Ember marked the edges by scuffing the hard dirt on either side.

"Duck to my height," she offered, then stepped aside without taking her eyes off the gap or her fingers from its edge, willing it to stay open.

Seth stomped through, throwing her one last sneer on his way out. She felt his passing in the soft compression of her lungs, as if he'd stolen a bit of her breath. The second Halfer passed and Ember sucked in air, trying to expand her ribcage as she worked to hold the opening steady, to maintain her focus so it didn't slam down between bodies - or worse, though one.

"What in the verge is going on here?"

A voice Ember didn't recognize as a Halfer's sent tremors through her muscles. Her eyes widened, but she couldn't take them off the Veil, the edges responding to her split mind and wobbling beneath her hold.

"Run." Chase's order sent the next three Halfers through in quick succession, each stealing more of her oxygen.

A scream grabbed Ember's attention, and she risked a glance, then refocused on the barrier as it shuddered against her negligence.

The last Halfer was being held back, pulling for the opening as a human seized her, their mouth pulled into a feral sneer.

What shattered her the most was finding Aaron's eyes stuck on her and the job she struggled to finish.

A punch hit its mark somewhere behind her, and it was impossible to tell which male produced the broken grunt and stumbling steps. Ember fought to keep focus as the last Halfer stumbled through, making it to freedom. Ripping her hand away, she recognized too late that she'd been reckless. The barrier shut on the girl's pack, shredding the outer pocket open. She sprinted into the trees after the other escapees.

The older human slammed against the invisible wall next to Ember. She scrambled back, flinching when she caught the edge of a pine that straddled Trifecta and the rest of the forest.

The man's fists pounded on the solid air, matching the furious beat of her own heart.

"No!" he shouted, then turned on Ember, using his larger body to grab her and shove her against the barrier. Red-rimmed eyes met hers, an anger in them that was alarmingly familiar despite the fact that she had never seen this man before.

"Tell me, little bitch, is Brandt out there, too? Did you throw him out again?"

Again?

"Kyle!" Aaron appeared over one of the man's shoulders while Chase grabbed the opposite arm. They both pulled Kyle back, and Ember struggled to inhale into her aching, fear-frozen lungs. The other human was on the ground, glaring at Chase as he slowly worked his jaw, the bright red mark promising a much darker bruise later.

"What the hell, Aaron? You saw it, you saw her! She did it. She had to. She needs to tell me where my son is right now!"

Ember shuddered, focusing on Chase, whose body trembled as he condemned Aaron with a poisonous glare. Her human friend was pale, eyes gone large and wild, as if in shock over his two worlds colliding at the worst possible time.

As the bruised human rose to his feet, Ember pressed against the barrier, shoulders to her ears, her fingers curling in as the truth settled in. The Fae weren't all she had to worry about anymore.

11

NICU

icu filled his lungs with the crisp cool atmosphere of the forest, letting his breath out slowly to lessen the mist cloud easing from his parted lips. He ran amid six other Fae; the air saturated with early morning quiet, broken only by the chirps of the birds and squirrels setting up for deeper winter.

Fae footsteps fell with the sound of a breeze. No words were spoken. They did not discuss strategies for the day's tasks, or how to portray gained knowledge to the council upon return.

The hunters might be keeping silent solely because of his presence, yet their steady and consistent movements spoke of familiarity. Eyes forward and softly focused, they did not share glances or steal looks at him. They were in their groove, ready for their day, pressing onward to compensate for time lost while the council sidelined Altaya.

This was Fae camaraderie. Though Terraborn, they were pure and unmarred, given a task that supported the Fae's presence here in Terra. They were aligned in their duty, focused on the result. There wasn't a need to discuss what came next, or to argue over what was best for themselves or for the Fae because it was all the same.

Today, Nicu had been granted the gift of being part of that. He took a moment to measure the Fate energies that followed him, finding them at the same low activation as they'd been all morning. As long as they remained aware but tame, he could ignore them and let himself enjoy these moments of being on a team of eager providers, rather than reluctant defenders.

The Fae had traps set along the north-northwestern quadrant of Trifecta. The hunting grounds spanned between both human and Fae lands. Their activities were approved via the Laws of Convergence, provided the Fae shared the game with the humans. A certain quota would be delivered per that agreement, then the rest could be kept or traded at the market.

Most of the traps had been tripped, but were barren. They gained one badger early on. As their bags remained empty, whispers began about organizing a hunt with another group to find some deer, elk, or the elusive mountain goat who preferred the cliff sides on Witch land, but sometimes came onto the lower slopes for foraging.

Nicu found more traces of humans than the hunters did of the game. Trampled undergrowth, cooked animal bones left behind from a quick lunch, even a fire ring that looked as if they planned to return soon. The discovery was unsettling, particularly considering the time of year. When the signs came too close to the traps, the Fae moved them to a different place, knowing animals would be more likely to avoid spaces with human scent.

"What are you doing?" Altaya approached Nicu as he scuffed a human-made trail deeper into the growth. This one led to a fire ring, which Nicu had rebuilt, so the stones sat in a compact circle, supported with earth to keep sparks from escaping out the bottom.

"Reinforcing the paths that will keep the humans away from what they are searching for." Nicu studied the semi-cleared path, then tapped his shoes against a nearby boulder to clear out the treads.

"Another kind of trap," Altaya noted, nodding with understanding. "We would have dispersed everything, making it harder to find. So there are benefits to spending so much time near gulls."

"The council isn't prone to assigning useless tasks."

"There is no offense in my words." Altaya lifted their hands, palms up. "We recognize the shame and the necessity in your team's assignment. It is a great thing you do for the Fae."

Nicu's silence held acceptance and thanks.

"With you and Branna reassigned, will Edan break from his mission to follow the Trimarked Child?"

Nicu stilled, wondering if the question had been planted within the hunter's mind. Had Wist requested they ask at an opportune time? Or was this mere curiosity aimed at the most secretive group amongst the Terraborn Fae?

"It is not necessary." A truthful answer, one that brought Altaya's focus on him. He hadn't fully realized until that moment how the hunter had separated their attention between the hunters under their command and Nicu. Now that he held Altaya's full awareness, he appreciated the skill that had likely secured their position as hunting party lead.

The universe decided to supply Altaya with an immediate example of why Edan was not needed at Ember's side. Nicu's world shifted beneath his feet, metaphysical taking over the physical for him alone. Fate Magic flared to life, brightening the day only for Nicu's eyes. Trees blurred to the right. The space he occupied swept left. His knees collapsed, and he found himself kneeling on the actual ground of Terra against the wave of angry energy.

Promise Magic pressed in, gleeful at the loosening of its bonds. A break had been made, a conduit opened. Nicu gripped the power within his chest, holding it in with his breath as he rearranged the meaning. There was no violation, only a mistake. The moment already passed, the Trimarked Child stepping away and back into line.

Fate rumbled with defiance, its presence a storm on the edges of his awareness. Yet, when Nicu ensured it no Promise had been broken, the force acquiesced, though the tension in its compliance warned him that its patience was finite.

When he looked up, he found the hunters standing as statues, bows drawn. Five arrows pointed at the forest surrounding them. Altaya held their bow loose at their side.

"The danger is not here," Nicu assured them. He pushed to his feet even as the Fae lowered their weapons, looking at him in askance. Nicu hesitated a moment, then met Altaya's eyes.

"I do not want to be in contempt of the Fae," he spoke. "I do not wish that for you, either."

"Speak plainly."

Nicu paused at the request, surprised it came from a Fae. With his hesitation, Altaya's grip on their bow tightened. They were not used to being questioned.

"You asked why Edan would not be connecting with The Trimarked Child. It is unnecessary because I can monitor her from afar."

"She has caused trouble."

Nicu breathed in through his nose. A full explanation would be unavoidable if he wanted to leave, and he needed to be moving already.

"She has come into contact with Center's boundary."

The Fae turned toward him, lips parted to take in a rush of air as if in tandem. Nicu ignored them, knowing Altaya was the one to convince.

There was one rule Ember had never broken, no matter how rebellious she felt. Never cross onto Fae land. That she had now was a greater concern than Wist's test, or the humans' change in behavior.

Protecting Ember made sense toward his goal of safeguarding the Fae. Nicu believed he could keep the two from ever crossing paths. Why would she take this risk? Why today, when he was finally awarded a position on a regular patrol?

She could not know, of course, yet Nicu still felt the twist of acidic resentment. Why couldn't she remain Underground for once? Keeping busy and out of sight as he'd envisioned when he'd asked Chase to include her among the Halfers.

Unless Chaos and Fate had a hand in this as well. Which meant none of his duties could fail today.

"The effort to contain the humans must continue even as the Trimarked Child must be attended to," Nicu stated. "You have seen what I have done for the human presence. I'm sure your unit can duplicate my efforts."

Altaya glanced over at their team, one brow bending with indecision. A quick shake of their head indicated a decision had been made, but it did not align with Nicu's.

"You have spent time with the hunters. It is the hunters' turn to spend time with the guardian."

Nicu took in a deep breath, prepping his body for movement while shifting uncertainties in his mind. Was Altaya walking a line, or drawing one? Was this pure curiosity to experience the responsibilities of a guardian? Or had the Council given orders Nicu was not privy to? Their willingness to abandon a directive spoke toward the later.

He let go of misgivings as he launched into a sudden sprint. The surrounding Fae did the same, falling in behind him. Altaya had been accepting and generous. There was no reason to question motives, but enough suspicion to remain alert. For now, the focus must be on his task.

Ember had not fully crossed the boundary, at least, allowing him a small measure of calm. Even so, a brush was way too close and clearly forbidden. Was she in trouble or being reckless? Nicu had to collect her answer. The Fae would then witness him. He would have to choose his words well, pull on all his skills to maintain balance on a day the Fate Magics were unusually active.

With Nicu in the lead, they arrived at the point of the breach. The Trimarked Child was no longer present. He discarded the simple theories. She was not walking in a distracted manner or waiting defiantly with sudden knowledge or demands. She was not there to answer for her transgression.

Nicu reluctantly yielded to Altaya, who bent to study the ground. The hunter was the superior tracker, yet Nicu was not used to another leader assuming responsibility in his missions. If Altaya noted his hesitation, they gave no indication as they picked up a dried, broken twig, then looked to the side. After stepping backward two times, they stopped again.

"The trodden path toward the boundary is scattered and uneven, as if she slid or tripped, though there is no object that would cause such a misstep. She was not alone. Over here, there are signs of a group walking three people side by side, with the total number remaining unclear. There is some unevenness that would support a theory that someone pushed her."

Altaya dropped the twig and watched how it fell. "Is that enough to satisfy?"

The hunter did not meet Nicu's gaze, giving away more than they liked. So, this was a test after all, but of what sort? An analysis of his loyalty, or simply his methods?

If the question regarding satisfaction had come from Edan, or Branna, then the response might be yes. Since the inquiry came from Altaya, Nicu could not let understanding be enough.

"Pushed or not, we will have the answer from the Trimarked Child herself."

Altaya nodded, then walked in a small circle around the disturbed ground.

"That way."

The hunter pointed across human lands, away from both Witch and Fae. Nicu drew a line with his mind, his shoulders stiff. He knew the location as one Chase and Ember visited on occasion. The very spot Nicu had sent Chase when he'd wanted the Halfer to meet the hybrid girl. He'd limited his knowledge of what they did there to guesses, not wanting to know too much so the truth was easier to keep from the Fae.

If he followed, that certainty may no longer be hidden from not only himself, but from the six Fae with him.

If he didn't follow, Altaya would assume there was something to hide. Whether they truly welcomed him or not, any lack of urgency on his part would be worthy of reporting to the council.

Pushed, fallen, or scrambling, Ember had brushed the Fae boundary. This task could not be delayed or left unfinished. Dread turned acidic behind his ribs, burning through his stoic certainty. For a moment, he missed his own team, then remembered it no longer existed.

The back of Nicu's neck itched where the Trimark medallion rested, as if asking him if its time had come. Gentle wisps of Wish Magic filtered his vision, the second of the Fate Magics to make an appearance today. Thankfully, the other Fae appeared blind to the energy. It wasn't enough to force Nicu's hand, but enough to remind him there was one piece of Aaron's wish to save Ember left to spend.

The omens gathered like a flock of crows, circling as they waited for the moment they could claim their prize.

"We must move faster."

His words were an order and a warning. Nicu's tattoos flared against his skin, opening up to absorb the flowing energy of the Fae's border alarm. He reclaimed a small amount of the power, directing the magic to flow over the ground. It bonded with the traces of Ember from where she'd fallen and crushed the undergrowth, recalling a spell he'd used once before to track down his troublesome ward, trusting that magic would be enough to get him to her in time.

12

EMBER

"**S**o Brandt was right." Spittle exited with Kyle's words, his body shaking as Aaron held him back. Chase had released his grip, edging closer to Ember, who silently wished the Veil's power would consume her once more, rendering her as invisible as the barrier itself.

"Is this what happened to all the runaways?" The guy on the ground scrambled to his feet, his injured chin darkening in increments. "You threw them off the edge? Left the rest of us here to rot?"

"It's not like that—"

The bruised boy rushed forward, but Chase was there to block him.

"Paul!" Aaron shouted, wrestling to hold Kyle back. "Stop it. She's stopped."

"Stopping is not the point! How many are missing because of her? Why them? Why not humans? What gives her the right to decide?"

Ember flinched away from the growl in his voice, his truth settling like ash in her stomach.

"Perhaps it's because the Halfers are the only ones who recognize her worth—who dared to see her at all," Chase retorted. Like this was on purpose. Was he trying to escalate this fight?

Kyle shifted his attention from Ember to Chase with his red-rimmed eyes.

"You're a Halfer? Is Brandt with you? Or did she toss him out?"

Chase's jaw tightened, his nostrils flared, as if he struggled against the man's presence and his own response to it.

"Anyone whose parents use them as a punching bag is welcome with the Halfers," he answered without saying.

"So he's there!" Kyle fought against Aaron again, his movement quick. Aaron shifted his grip quickly, pulling Kyle back into unwilling submission. "I want to see him—"

Chase barked out a harsh bite of laughter. "No."

"Who do you think you are? How dare you keep my son away from me!"

"Seems to me you did that just fine on your own."

Ember wondered if moving in with the Halfers would have saved the boy who tried to kill her, or if his attitude toward her would have ended with them in the same situation. The Halfers might have rescued him from a violent home, but as Seth showed, that didn't guarantee any greater tolerance for the Trimarked Child.

Either way, it didn't matter. Their lives had entangled in the worst of ways, and even with him gone, it appeared she still had consequences to pay.

"Chase." Aaron shook his head, leaning back as his arms strained against Kyle's pull. "This isn't helping."

"Not my problem."

"Aaron, you know them?" Paul demanded, shouting over Chase, who shrugged and moved a step nearer to Ember while the humans were focused on Aaron.

"I told you, I talked to Ember—"

"By name." Paul gaped. "And him?"

"Kind of fell into that one," Aaron said.

"What the fades does that mean?"

"You wanted me to investigate." Aaron's voice softened, carrying a note of regret that stripped away its usual authority.

Paul shook his head, then noticed that Chase was sidling toward Ember and took a threatening step forward.

"Are you trying to get her to let you out before we settle this?" The human's lips curled in disdain as he strode between Chase and Ember. Aaron shifted to position himself on the other side of Kyle, an empty vocalization directed at Paul.

"Why doesn't she just throw herself out?" Kyle asked.

The humans stopped, noting how Ember was pressed against the barrier, caught between it and too many angry people to make a solid run for it.

"You don't understand," Ember answered, hoping Kyle's logical question meant someone might listen. "It's hard. Dangerous. Those who agree recognize the risks—"

"Of what? Freedom?"

"Of being cut in half." Chase thrust a finger toward the fabric and food fragments the barrier had sliced through when the last Halfer barely made it out. Ember winced, but didn't defend herself by saying she'd never killed anyone before. She'd never let so many out before, either. And if the humans forced her to attempt a mass exodus ... It was better they had Chase's imagery.

Paul shook his head, as if deciding Chase's claim was a lie. He stared pointedly at Aaron, who still held Kyle back. Aaron flinched, releasing the older man, but stepped into a position that blocked him from reaching her. Paul crossed his arms, his stance rigid.

"How friendly are you with them, exactly?" Paul spat out the word 'them,' like he'd meant vermin. "Will you be able to do what needs to be done?"

"What are you talking about?" Aaron asked, his head tilted at a cautious angle.

"Take them back to town. To Janice and your Dad. They're better at this, and can convince them to talk."

Ember eyed the space between the people in front of her. Paul stood too close to Chase for her to attempt an escape to the left, or straight ahead. Right, there was the tree she'd run into, but the challenge was Aaron, who was within lunging distance.

Would he let her pass? He was clearly trying to make peace with the humans. Apologizing for knowing her and Chase. Releasing Kyle when given a pointed look. Sure, he'd moved so Kyle couldn't grab her immediately, but maybe her assumption was wrong. He might want to keep her there, believing that if they worked through this mess, then everyone would eventually just go home.

Stupid optimistic puppy dog boy.

A soft tickle edged into the peripheral of Ember's senses, bringing with it the scent of pine and mist.

There would be no running now.

Ember rose to her toes, trembling as she pressed herself into the invisible energy. Though she couldn't detect any movement, the threat of them might encourage the humans to leave. To limit the number of battles she needed to fight. She caught Chase's attention.

"Nicu."

"Verge," Chase cursed.

"What's happening?" Aaron asked, as if he deserved to sound concerned.

"A Fae is coming." Ember curled her lips at the humans in front of her, not sparing Aaron with her glare.

"Verge," Paul echoed Chase, spinning to look into the trees. "Her fading guardian."

"The Fae?" Kyle gasped, stumbling backward, his chest heaving. His pupils dilated, and the color drained from his cheeks. "The memory stealers? They're worse than the damn Witches taking over my factory, stealing my job. Witches are at least open thieves. The Fae take what's inside you. What are we going to do?"

Ember recognized the echo of Susan in Kyle's rant and recoiled from the picture he painted of the Fae. Yes, they were dangerous, but she couldn't quite relinquish the hope that Nicu came to lambaste the humans. That he'd lecture her about being reckless, then walk away. Again.

Chase pulled in closer to the group, also looking into the trees. He kept his voice low, hoping Nicu was still too far away to hear them speak.

"Don't tell the Fae what you saw."

Paul twisted to show Chase his sneer. "You think you can order me around?"

Chase shrugged. "They already have a reason to take her. If you give them another one, you won't even have the chance to drag her back to Town."

Pine and mist swamped Ember's senses. Nicu seemed to materialize out of the forest, the skin of his cheekbones pulled tight. Tattoos crawled up his neck and over his exposed hands. Behind him, six Fae showed themselves just enough to make it clear each one of them had arrows drawn.

He brought the Fae?

Ember's eyes fluttered closed. Her frantic heartbeat slowed, sinking into a heavy, burdened rhythm.

"This is no business of yours, Fae." Paul's words shot through the air and Ember winced away from the force.

"The Trimarked Child is my concern," Nicu countered. "She has attempted to cross the Fae boundary."

Ember opened her gray eyes and met Nicu's amber stare head-on. If she could see his thoughts, she'd find the moment he'd chosen. The second he decided. Not that it mattered. It couldn't matter.

Silly girl, letting a Fae break your heart.

No, never her heart. Only her trust.

Her gaze darted to Chase, who'd had drawn himself up,

eyes narrowed onto the Fae, his thin-lipped frown betraying his own disappointed surprise.

Anger flushed Ember's cheeks and magical power generated from her bones, surging to her fingertips, threatening to spark. She held it back, but for what? Caught between the humans who saw her open the barrier and the Fae who came because four fingers crossed their border, what did she have to lose?

Susan's image flooded Ember's thoughts, and she sucked in a breath, retracting the energy wanting to burst through her. She swallowed a hot bubble of laughter. Look at that control! If he wasn't here to capture her, Nicu might actually be proud.

The ache at Ember's sternum deepened as she grasped for the vocabulary required to fix the situation. She needed the ideal argument, the flawless response—but the truth settled heavy: no words would ever be perfect enough.

This wasn't just trouble. It was the kind that left scars.

"An accident," Chase spoke up for her. "We were walking, and I knocked her into the barrier. So blame me."

"The rule is for her," Nicu countered.

"It was half a second," Chase shot back.

Nicu blinked, but Ember wasn't fluent in Fae body language, leaving her unable to decipher the meaning behind that particular lowering of his lids.

"There, now you know," Paul inserted himself, his voice overloud in an attempt to hide the quiet tremor. "You have no claim. We do. Go away."

"Claim to what?" Nicu's eyes tightened. Ember recognized that one. He was not happy that a human dared to speak to him, especially about Ember. Or that he basically shouted to the Fae that they were keeping secrets.

"This happened on human land." Aaron's low, base tone surprised Ember. His chest puffed out in a way she hadn't seen since the first time he squared off against Chase.

Was he claiming her? To protect her as a friend, or to set her up to be taken by the humans?

Did it matter if it got Nicu to walk away?

"Just what occurred here?" A new voice, but also familiar. Ember studied the speaker's features, her throat tightening as she realized this was the second time this particular Fae had pointed an arrow at her face.

"It's not Fae concern." Aaron's clipped words held an authority Ember hadn't heard since their semi-disastrous meeting when he'd demanded her help to find Nicu. The soccer captain was asserting his jurisdiction over what he considered his side of the pitch.

"We will decide that." Nicu stepped forward as if to claim Ember.

"No." Though he shook like a leaf, Kyle blocked Nicu's path, his shoulders high and his fists clenched at his hips. "I know the Laws of Convergence, pixie. The Trimarked bitch is on human land, in our custody. If you want to collect her, you'll need to send one of your Elders to negotiate."

Aaron rushed to Ember's side. The hand he wrapped around her bicep was gentle.

"Let's get you out of here," he whispered. She gaped at him, brows furrowed with disbelief.

"Let go," she snapped, trying to yank her arm free. Aaron scanned the faces surrounding them, then shook his head.

"Paul, we need to take her to the Town Hall with Kyle."

"That will not happen." Nicu's voice had dropped an octave, along with his chin. He glowered at Aaron, daring him to disagree.

Ember's wide eyes locked onto Chase, yet he remained in place, his hands at his side shifting between flexed and fisted. His attention was solidly on the threat that was Nicu, offering her no help or guidance.

Filling her lungs with crisp air, Ember accepted what had

to happen next. Between human hands and Fae arrows, she would have to test her luck with the humans.

Aaron shifted Ember toward Paul, but she jerked her arm free, glaring at him.

"I can walk," she insisted. Aaron frowned, but waved off Paul's frustrated grasping.

"One of you will remain here," Nicu demanded, regaining the attention he'd lost. "We will discuss exactly how long you expect to keep the Trimarked Child away from us."

Aaron paused a moment, then nodded.

"I'll stay. Paul, take her to Town Hall with Kyle. If my dad isn't there, find him. I'll catch up as soon as I can."

Paul's face darkened as if he repressed a rude retort. He reached for Ember, who sidestepped his grasp with little difficulty, keeping her eyes toward the ground to make it seem like she hadn't noticed him at all.

As they walked away, her footsteps much quieter than the two hulking humans who flanked her, Ember struggled to breathe her emotions into submission. She wanted to believe Aaron's flat tone was all show. That he was still a misguided friend who believed that peace was an option. But a golden-eyed Fae had left her tattered, with hope hanging in frayed, worthless threads.

13

NICU

A heavy beat thrummed against Nicu's temples, deep and dangerous. This situation was not in his control, an unfortunate truth that ached in the space behind his brow. There were too many moving pieces. Too many human eyes. Too many Fae.

Emotions boiled within his blood and Nicu forced them into submission. Now was not the moment to weigh and judge wounds. He needed his thoughts clear.

Nicu watched the Trimarked Girl march away, jerking her arm out of the younger human's grip each time he tried to get a hold of her. With every step she took, another piece of Promise Magic frayed.

Was this because of her recklessness? Had she let herself become too visible? Or had he arrived too late, with too large of an audience?

He needed a chance to gather from the edges, letting patience steer the game. To move in increments that did not trigger the constrictive web of Fate Magic. The hunters behind him expected a more decisive approach, and Nicu must give that impression.

Nicu longed to have Branna at his side rather than Altaya.

He needed access to Edan's well of secrets. Yet wishes were not his to claim. As if to drive that point home, the wisps of Wish Magic vanished, signaling their tie was to Ember, and not him.

All he had were the two males before him and the information they withheld.

"Explain yourselves," he ordered.

The Halfer's cheeks flushed with anger, his lips thinned against his secrets. Green eyes with a hint of fine cut gem roved over each of the Fae.

"I think it's been explained," Chase drawled. "You've been outmaneuvered by a colony of gulls."

Irritation warred with relief. Chase would do his job and remain unhelpful, which would buy Nicu time to assess the circumstances before Altaya's presence forced him into action. He turned to Aaron. Had the human existed in their world long enough to understand the rules? Perhaps a blunt strategy would foster the defiance Nicu needed from him.

"What is her crime against your people?"

Aaron scowled and shook his head.

"Not your business. I'm just here to figure out if you're sending this Elder to negotiate."

"And I want to know what either of you think you're going to do with Ember." Chase's addition drifted beneath the tension, providing it with a solid base to stand on. His intent to protect Ember was clear in the wide flex of his fingers.

Nicu's eyes were sharp, studying the half-human's responses. Questions rose unbidden. Why were they lingering on the edge of Trifecta? Why had they found so many footsteps at the Fae border, yet only Chase stood here? It seemed unlikely the humans traveled with them, though one group might have followed the other.

Puzzle pieces tried to fit together in Nicu's mind. Conjecture against fact. Promise Magic wrapped around each potential image, trying to force a complete picture. He mentally swatted it away. He'd spent too much time cultivating what he knew and what he didn't to accept mere assumptions.

Assuming was dangerous. It could tip the scales of Fate magic, allowing it to burst free in the direction Nicu's will lead. Toward himself, or toward Ember. Which of them Fate magic tore apart rested solidly within the confines of his willpower.

Today was not a good day to run with the Fae, after all.

"Do the Halfers have any claim here?" Nicu hoped for an answer without any weight. A hint at what had occurred that left the hunters questioning the relevance.

The Halfer did not comply. "No more than either of you. If she was any other human—"

"She is not."

Nicu cut off each word. As if inspired by his tone, Altaya lowered their bow and moved forward to stand beside him.

"Huh." Chase clicked his tongue. "You won't pry anything out of them, Aaron. Run along to chase after your friends. That girl had better not get hurt. Do you understand me?"

Aaron scowled. Whether in response to Chase's order or to the insinuation that he would let Ember be harmed, Nicu wasn't certain.

He surmised that the Halfer believed Ember safer with the humans than with the Fae. That Chase interpreted Altaya's movement as a sign this meeting needed to end. He was fulfilling his purpose as a layer of protection around Ember, forcing Nicu to back away without betraying their connection.

"This is only a temporary deflection," Nicu warned Chase. The bold statement served as a consolation for the Fae accompanying him as he directed their retreat. Altaya raised a brow in question, but followed his example. After a few paces, Nicu turned and led the Fae deeper into the trees.

The confrontation had gone horribly. Though Nicu's connections to Aaron and Chase remained secret, he'd clearly backed down without gaining any helpful information. As parting threats went, the one he'd delivered had been insubstantial.

The Fae hindered Nicu in ways he had not anticipated, and by the look on the lead hunter's face, they expected an explanation.

"What is going on?" Altaya demanded once they were out of earshot. They stopped the party in their tracks by planting their own feet and forcing Nicu to face them. "You ran like Chaos was chasing you to get to her, then you let her walk away with the humans?"

"They invoked the Laws of Convergence." Nicu's reminder should have been unnecessary.

Altaya frowned. "I understand why the Trimarked was allowed to leave. But why not press those last two for more information?"

Nicu checked in on his physical response, ensuring his shoulders remained low and his breathing even. Wist's training had been harsh, yet it would be exactly what carried Nicu through this argument. Altaya was too wild, too free with their responses. Nicu embodied control.

"I will not waste my time collecting lies when there are more efficient ways toward the truth."

"Spying?"

"Edan's specialty." Nicu imagined Branna's glare would be volcanic if she knew he'd invoked their lost comrade. Yet alluding to the secretive Fae had the desired effect. Altaya drew in a calming breath, glancing around the forest as if they might catch the elusive Fae hiding in the foliage.

"You will get a message to him?"

"Not necessary. His task was to spy on the humans. With his skill, it is unlikely he'd miss the Trimarked Child's presence."

Altaya tilted their head as they absorbed this version of the truth Nicu fully believed; otherwise, he would not have been able to produce the words.

Though Edan's spirit was separate from his body, he was connected to Branna, who had been sent to Town. Even in his current form, he was more than capable of collecting secrets. Everything Nicu shared with Altaya was not only possible, but likely.

"Then we return to Center and inform the Elders," Altaya directed.

Nicu faced Center as if in thought. Promise magic pooled at the base of his spine, burning against the nerves.

"That is not advisable."

"Because you refuse to admit to a mistake," Altaya assumed.

"They will ask questions to which we do not have answers. They will want to know if the Remembrance Spell has been breached. If the Trimarked Child has shown evidence of power, and if this has impacted the humans directly or indirectly. Trust that these explanations are best gathered before we return to Center."

Altaya's skin darkened. Their eyes flickered between the other hunters, Nicu, and toward Fae land.

"There has been a heaviness in the air all day."

Nicu's slow blink swallowed his flinch. "Yes."

There was no point in denying a fact.

"I cannot sense it fully. I can only assume this is Promise Magic. You say she may have affected the humans. Could something she did have triggered its presence? Why do you not find security within Center? Why not let her break it?"

"Do you know the cost of a failed Promise?" Nicu's quiet question settled beneath the sounds of creaking branches and the chatter of early winter forest creatures.

"She will die." Stated simply. As if Ember's life had no more value than her namesake—something to burn while useful, then extinguished to prevent any lingering threat. As if she wasn't the only one at risk.

"It is not a true death," Nicu countered. "The universal

power will scatter her atoms back into the universe as the cost for breaking the Promise. Or it will do so to me."

"What have you done to break it?"

"It is more an issue of what I do not do."

"You mean we have to make sure she is the one to renege. That you do the bare minimum so Fate does not claim you. And then you can be free of this. Free to be Fae again."

Nicu stood steadfast. That was Altaya's truth and he let them have it. The image was beautiful, certainly. No longer torn between duties. Have more days filled with certainty and honorable work, as this morning had been.

But his dedication to preserve balance would not bend. As long as the Promise Magic did not break, he could repair it. Stability could be maintained.

"Let us dispatch a scout to alert the council." Altaya selected one with a small gesture. "Then you can do what is needed."

Nicu tilted his head to the left, signaling disagreement. "If you send a harbinger of Chaos, they will not thank you for it."

Altaya shook their head, and the chosen messenger returned to formation. Their dark eyes shifted to a deeper hue. The conversation didn't sit well with the hunter. Altaya had likely never questioned the best way to serve the Fae.

"Tell me your plan." Altaya's magic grew from the ground. Invisible energy prickled at Nicu's skin as it wrapped around his ankles and trailed up his body, aiming for his throat. A revelation spell.

He could not blame them, engaged with a Fae known to practice deceptive truths. Nicu's answers would bring doubt to the strength of his loyalties, or to where they lay. The truth wouldn't satisfy them, which was precisely why he could not allow his defenses to fall.

Nicu faced the hunter, allowing them to sense their own spell reach for its purpose. His tattoos swarmed upward, wrapping around his neck as Altaya's magic made contact. Living

Ink darkened with power, neutralizing its intent. Nicu held on to the energy even as the Ink settled into its passive state. At rest, his tattoos were aligned, parallel, but never intertwined, an echo of his place amongst the Fae.

Altaya's lips parted. They took a small step back at Nicu's easy display. So they had not known the full extent of his mutations. Now they did.

Nicu waited while Altaya's understanding adjusted to this new information. Their dark eyes widened as the puzzle pieces fell together. Ember's untested power. His ability to take it. He let go of the magic in that moment, releasing it back into the land surrounding them while he met the hunter's direct gaze and gave the only answer that mattered.

"I am her guardian for a reason."

14

EMBER

*E*mber grit her teeth when Paul's toes scraped against her heels for the third time. She shot an elbow back without any strength behind it. He fell for the feint and dodged to the side, his reaction instant and his feet quick.

These soccer boys really needed to leave her alone.

"Where is Brandt?" Kyle fell into step beside her and Ember jumped. She hadn't forgotten about him. It was just Paul seemed the one more willing to get near her.

"Aaron said he asked you once," Kyle revealed. "If Brandt was in the tunnels. He said you didn't know. Did you lie to him?"

Aaron said what?

Ember clenched her fists against her thighs, refusing to answer either of their questions. They appeared to have plenty of information already.

What was Aaron doing, discussing her with other humans? What else had he said?

No. She wouldn't allow any more shattered hope or broken expectations. She'd been right to keep her walls up, to hold him at a distance. Just this morning, he had been talking about Brandt. Had that been his goal all along? Had he stayed close only to gather something useful to share with the humans?

He's not that good an actor.

Really? Because this forced march into Town that he organized suggested otherwise.

Heavy and steady footfalls alerted her that the traitor had arrived. When he fell in beside them, he wasn't even winded.

"When I said I'd catch up, it didn't mean you had to walk so slow." Aaron glanced between the two humans and Ember, as if trying to read the tone of their interaction.

"You're just that quick." Paul grinned, slapping a palm against Aaron's shoulder. Ember didn't miss the brief glance he sent toward her or the smirk that followed.

Fading boys marking their territory.

The way Aaron twisted away left Ember's heart thudding in her chest, but she swallowed hard on the spark of hope that threatened to catch fire.

"So what did you learn?" Paul asked. "You didn't give that Fae any promises, did you?"

"Of course not," Aaron assured him. "It was a lot of staking a claim on Ember, and a warning not to hide her. Basically, the Fae won't come for her immediately, but they are not letting go of their intention to question her about the border breach."

"If everything goes right, they won't get that chance." Paul's words might have sounded supportive on their own, but the wild gleam in his eyes suggested his plans didn't prioritize Ember's safety.

"What does that mean, Paul? What do you want from her, exactly?"

"She needs to tell us where Brandt is!" Kyle's shout cut through the air, and Aaron flinched. The sound clearly struck more than his ears—his shoulders tensed, and a flicker of frustration crossed his face. Knowing Aaron, he'd been working to keep the situation calm, but Kyle's outburst made it obvious Aaron's efforts to maintain peace were slipping out of reach.

"This is bigger than that," Paul argued. "She was letting people out. We don't have to be trapped anymore, but she hasn't said a fading word about offering us our freedom."

"Did Brandt ask to leave?" Kyle's question was quiet and heavy. Aaron exhaled, his shoulders sagging under the weight of the moment. He studied Ember who pursed her lips and turned her face away.

"She isn't talking." Paul stated the obvious. "Let's get her to your dad, like you said. I want out of this pixie-infested forest."

"They can't take her," Kyle asserted. "I invoked the Laws of Convergence. They have to send an Elder and those old bastards never leave Center."

"Don't underestimate Nicu," Aaron muttered, his gaze scanning the trees before settling on Ember.

"Give us a minute," he told the humans, hauling her up the hill.

"Aaron, what in the verge —"

"Paul, I said wait!"

Paul stepped back in surprise, then crossed his arms, frowning as he gave a small nod. Kyle looked between them with a deep crease between his brows, but didn't look inclined to walk toward the Fae.

"You really can't run." Aaron spoke as if he felt sorry for her. As if he wished she could. "Nicu is pissed. Even if you reach The Circle, without Leona, can you trust that they'll protect you against both the Fae and humans? And the Halfers —"

"I get it." Ember grit her teeth, wishing that covering her ears wasn't considered a childish thing to do. Fades, she'd lived all those examples today. She didn't need to hear him spell it out. "I'm walking, aren't I?"

Aaron's lips thinned, and he directed his fierce gaze at Ember.

"What were you thinking?"

Ember fought against the burn in her eyes. Aaron had never sounded this angry, his eyes dark and unyielding.

"Same as always. Paying Chase back for room and board."

"He should fading know better, too." Aaron took a deep breath. "Em, I can't save you from this one."

"Is that what you're trying to do?"

Aaron's brow creased, and he straightened his back. "Of course it is. What do you think—"

"You told them you've talked to me about Brandt."

"Because I was keeping them out of the Underground."

Naturally. He'd given her up to protect Chase, his precious coffee date.

"I see. So Chase might forgive you, at least."

"Forgive? Ember, what in the realms is happening?"

"You tell me, Aaron. How do they know we're connected? How is it that you had this convenient plan to send me into Town with them? And to your father!"

"Are you kidding me? We're friends, for verge sake. Why would you think that?"

Ember looked pointedly toward Paul and Kyle, then back to Aaron.

"I've saved you, Em. I brought Chase when Brandt had you. I followed you into a cave even though the Queen was there."

"So I'm in your debt now? Is this your way of making me repay you?"

Aaron's mouth widened in offense, his posture straightening with surprise.

"You had no right to mention me to anyone. I thought you understood. You said we're friends, but then—" Ember's throat closed on her words.

"That's not fair, Ember. I have been nothing but understanding, even with Bra—" Aaron glanced at the humans. "Stuff."

"Understanding?" Ember's silvery eyes hardened. "Aaron, you could never understand."

Ember's ears filled with the pressure of their silence. Aaron opened his mouth to speak a few times, then closed it quickly as if catching words he didn't want to spill out.

"What is taking so fading long?" Paul demanded.

"Nothing," Aaron called back, keeping his attention on Ember. "We can go now. I assumed she would talk to me. I was wrong."

Ember turned away, trudging down the hill and ignoring her escorts. Cold air filled her lungs through parted lips as she kept her eyes wide and dry, refusing to let anything that human boy said get under her skin.

15

TRISTAN

ristan leaned against the giant sequoia, not at all afraid that it would try to suck in his soul. Though the roots were raw and hungry, the trunk displayed some manners, behaving like a normal tree, except for when it was being fed.

Soon, he promised. Only a few more minutes of patience.

The wind rustled the pine boughs of the standing trees outside No Man's Land, yet not even a slight breeze trailed inside to ruffle the strands of Tristan's auburn hair. It hung to his shoulders at the moment, his black trilby hat suspended between open palms, fingers flicking against the brim every now and again to set it spinning.

A bird caught Tristan's eye, a bright red missile with beady eyes fixed upon him. It twisted to avoid outstretched branches and flapped its wings a few times to keep aloft amongst the inconsistent breeze.

While seeing a cardinal this time of year wasn't unusual, this bird defied nature. Instead of turning away from No Man's Land, it cut right into it. As it broke the barrier, the wizardry that held it together fell apart. What had appeared to be a bird proved to be a folded piece of cloth, now drifting toward the ground without the aid of magic to support its form.

Unable to cast within No Man's, Tristan crossed the distance with seven normal strides and caught the offering with long, steady fingers. He smoothed the trilby over his hair while holding the small square open in his left hand.

The sketch showed a pentacle framed by an intricate butterfly's wing on the right side, underlined in a simple sentence of flowing script.

The little Witch has the information you seek.

Did she now?

Tristan folded the cloth like any ordinary handkerchief and tucked it into the interior pocket that had once held a bowie knife.

A clever spell, Tristan wished the Work had one more message in it. It had taken shape over the last few days. First, he'd cloned a piece of Ember's coat after snagging a loose thread without her noticing. A strand of her hair was easy to pluck from its static connection to the back of her shoulder. Some water from The Circle and dirt from Center, all gathered at a speed that kept any mage from detecting his passage.

At the edge of the cave below No Man's, where all magics of the realm had been forced to coexist, he combined the ingredients. With the mixture prepared, he infused a simple request to locate the strongest traces of Veil magic beyond Ember.

Though the handkerchief was no longer useful, it had provided information that would hopefully lead to the next phase.

Tristan opened a path through time and space, entering The Circle in a handful of steps. He remained at the edges of the inhabited area, though he needn't have bothered. The Coven still wallowed from the loss of their High Priestess.

Her daughter was likely the most affected.

The Circle held no mystery for Tristan. As one of the earliest planners, he had been involved since the final Fade forced them through. The location of their artifacts—even the hidden ones—was no secret to him. He knew where they slept, where they worked, and the trivial projects they clung to in an attempt to feel valuable in this realm of humanity.

He knew exactly where the little Witch spent her time.

Tristan slowed at the back end of the warehouse buildings, settling into a non-magical pace. With silent steps, he remained as close to the corrugated steel walls as he could without dirtying his double-breasted wool coat.

"She has responsibilities!" someone shouted from the entrance. A Witch stormed away, the cherry color of her straight hair telling Tristan it was the Priestess Hannae. The temper tantrum let him know she had not found her quarry, and the aide following her used slower steps, seemingly eager to put distance between them.

Were they after the same Witch? Tristan hoped so.

He waited until the pair vanished from sight, making sure they didn't double back. Once certain the passage had cleared, he slipped around the corner, through the door, and shut it behind him faster than a human's blink.

An odd magic filtered through the air of the empty warehouse. Tristan took a moment to study it, startled when the sharp lines of its structure suggested something Fae, but not active. Perhaps there was an artifact nearby, though not one likely to cause trouble.

Tristan scanned the ample space, unwilling to trust appearances when the Witch he sought displayed such skill. Strange energy clung to the air, yet the room remained vacant. The main building's door stood solid and locked, and the blinds over the office window hung tightly shut. If she hid inside, it was likely from Priestess Hannae and her kind. Time might be short before she emerged, but it would prove enough.

Tristan made his way to the twin tables arranged to utilize

their doubled length, his natural pace carrying him to the empty seat. Cups of pencils and stacks of notebooks cluttered the surface, leaving only a clear spot directly in front of the chair.

Tristan placed his palm flat on the table where an open notepad would have fit perfectly.

Interesting, and hopefully not the reason he was here. Devi would likely keep the more important volumes close by. The first notebook he picked up had a green cover. He intended to flip through it, but his pace slowed after just a few pages. Spells for separation of physical materials down to the molecules. A time reversal component. And was that a spell or a chemistry equation?

Tristan caught himself studying for a minute too long and he slammed the book shut. There was no doubt the young Witch was clever. Too sharp for her, or any age. Had Leona—?

Not important.

Devi's skill was exciting in one aspect, though. The spell had been right. The little Witch had the information required. He only needed to find it.

Tristan skimmed each notebook and then placed them back exactly as he'd found them. So many spells and experiments. There were hundreds of pages Tristan would love to study later, as if she were his contemporary instead of his junior. Yet none of them applied to his needs. He slammed the book he'd just finished into place, glancing quickly toward those shaded windows in case the echo pulled out a Witch who may or may not be hiding there.

If she was, and the required information lay in the missing booklet, he might have to invade her space.

Tristan shelved the thought, at least while a few volumes remained to be searched. Further down the table than he expected to find it, he discovered a notebook far more worn than the others. He carefully slipped it from the bottom of the pile, balancing it against gravity as he noticed papers jutting out at odd angles with random pieces of paper tucked between them. Tristan skipped the first section and flipped to the end, where a few blank sheets held the rest of the book together.

This time, both corners of the Wizard's lips ticked upward.

Notes and a drawing.

Tristan scanned the script, traced the lines that expanded over multiple pages to get from point A to B.

It showed the physical and magical structure of the Trimarked Tattoo.

Tristan returned to the text, his breath held and his heartbeat thudding against the strain.

The Ink itself is worth more study, but progress must be slow. The Binding Ink ties the spell to Ember, but it does not end with her. It is connected elsewhere, possibly to multiple points. At this stage, I don't have sufficient evidence to suggest specifics, but based on what is known about her birth and the Fae, I suspect Nicu is one of the connections.

Ah. The stoic Fae was linked to his daughter, just as Tristan suspected. He had a moment of regret for not investigating the event of her birth. Though he didn't have that information, the Witch had at least given him a direction.

Even with trembling fingers, Tristan was careful to replace the book just so. Whenever Devi returned, she wouldn't suspect he'd paid her treasure trove a visit.

One step to the door and another through it. Four more took him deep into the forest, where he could pause.

He drew in a long breath of Terran air, imagining that he could taste the sweetness of Heldu at his edges. All his careful planning was paying off. The pieces were coming together. He could do this. In fact, he was going to. Once the Witches were back on Heldu, they'd see his methods were worth returning home. They'd recognize the hero he had become for them.

Only a few final actions remained before victory. Tristan needed the Trimarked medallion—the external piece of

Ember's Binding Spell. Just three days ago, he had seen the artifact tied and hidden beneath the braids of the Fae he had knocked out and dragged through Trifecta into No Man's Land. He left it behind, content with knowing where to find it.

Now it was Nicu's turn to prove himself useful at last.

16

EMBER

*T*own's lower end once thrived as a bustling downtown, but since the Convergence, only the hollow skeleton of a strip mall remained. The Trifectans had stripped the space bare, salvaging and repurposing what held value, discarding the rest. Now, empty booths and tables sat like forgotten relics, waiting for the Saturday markets to breathe life into them. The wind carried whispers through cracked storefronts, rattling rusted signs.

Paul led Ember and the others past the long, multi-entranced building until it broke away, revealing a wide driveway. Through the opening, Ember spotted a cluster of vehicles, their faded paint dulled by time. The electric models, gathered by the town council after the Convergence cut them off from the outside world, sat idle. Ember's stomach twisted. She had helped Chase install a virus in those cars months ago, an impulsive move that sparked the chain of events leading her to this moment.

Beyond the driveway, a red brick building jutted from the landscape, distinct against the strip mall's faded cream and brown tones. As they approached, the polished metal sign embedded in the masonry caught the faintest sliver of light, announcing the police station's presence. Paul reached for Ember's arm and she twisted out of the way, shaking her head. She refused to let him lead her like a captive, not when she had come willingly.

Paul scowled and his body stiffened as if he might pounce toward her. Aaron slipped between them and opened the door, gesturing Ember through with a slight roll of his eyes. If he meant the gesture as an olive branch, he could keep it.

Ember stepped inside and halted in the small entryway, unsure where they expected her to go. A high countertop stretched across the space, separating the rest of the interior. The word "Reception" was carved into the front in thick block letters, likely predating the Convergence. It was far too simple and plain to be crafted by a Fae.

Beyond the counter, three bulky metal desks faced forward, two on the left and another on the right. Behind the single silvery desk, a larger wooden one sat in a glass-walled space, separated from the rest of the building.

From within the enclosed office, Branna's gaze lingered too long, sharp and calculating, as if weighing Ember's mortality with quiet detachment.

Ember glanced at Aaron, who glowered at the female Fae, his eyes wide and lips thinned. Unhappy and surprised, so at least he wasn't expecting her.

Were they here for her? Had Nicu gotten word to Branna to reclaim Ember? Though not an Elder, the necromancer exuded an intimidating and dark power. Would the humans give in?

"What are they doing here?" Kyle snapped. "There's no way the Fae Council knows about us yet."

Ember shook her head, but stayed silent. The gull seemed to forget they were dealing with mages. Kyle's use of "they" let Ember notice another young Fae past Branna. He faced a human woman sitting at the desk, while a man at the far end observed the exchange with crossed arms. The man's attention shifted to them, and he spoke, though they couldn't hear the words from where they stood at the front of the office.

"Oh, good." Paul closed the door behind them with a hard click. "Coach is here. That will make this easier."

"Dad?" Aaron echoed as the glass door opened. The older man stepped out, his button-down shirt untucked from pleated khaki pants. His posture was perfect, his form well-defined under the fitted clothes.

So this must be Coach, Aaron's father, Ember thought.

"Gus," Kyle greeted, reaching over the counter to shake Coach's hand. Gus accepted the handshake even as his attention flickered over the four of them, returning to Aaron and Ember to study the two and the lack of inches between them.

Ember shifted, easing away to widen the narrow gap, but the door creaked open again as a fifth body pressed inside, leaving no space to maneuver. She kept her gaze forward, heart pounding, certain the greater threat stood in front of her with the human and the Fae in the office.

"Aaron, I hope this isn't your way of telling me the Trimarked Child is where your damned-good coffee came from," Gus said.

"That would be me," Chase raised a two-finger salute, his statement informing Ember he'd been the last person to squeeze inside.

Ember took advantage of Chase's distraction and managed a sidestep from the group, her back finding the wall. With the man behind the counter tracking her every move, Ember shifted casually, leaning against the white brick as if at ease. In reality, she edged away from the rising tension pressing in on everyone near the entry.

Gus' eyes snapped over to Chase as he let out a long breath between pursed lips, his arms pressed against the edge of the counter as if he might do an upright pushup, or launch himself over it.

"What the verge have you been doing?" Gus demanded of Aaron.

"What you asked of him," Chase drawled. "Find the Halfers. Got real close, too."

"Close enough to see the Trimarked girl throwing out— Ow!"

Kyle contracted, clutching his stomach, which had remained within reach of Chase's bony elbow. Ember tucked her hands underneath her arms. Her power had reacted to Kyle's partial statement, rising incrementally with each word, likely wanting to protect her, but threatening to expose her secret at the same time.

Funny how you still pretend it's a secret.

Ember scanned the crowd, gauging how far the door was. Reaching it meant pushing past at least one person. Her eyes flicked toward the office, assessing that gap as well, and she wondered who would reach her first—the humans or the Fae. With human reflexes and the Fae's speed, it was honestly a toss-up.

"What do you think you're doing?" Gus left his guarded spot behind the counter, stepping aside to utilize a hidden door at the far end before joining them in the already crowded space.

Ember blew out a hard breath, sweat gathering against her skin under the layers of her coat and sweater. She refused to remove them, though, rejecting the idea that she'd be inside for much longer. If Chase managed a big enough distraction, she'd take the chance and get the verge out.

"There are Fae here," Chase offered calmly. "I'm sure we can all agree they don't need the details of this discussion."

As all the humans looked toward the office, Ember grit her teeth. Why not telegraph the fact that they were talking about Branna and her companion? Though, to be honest, the Fae were probably reading their lips.

"They can't take her," Kyle insisted. "The Laws say she's ours."

"The Laws," Gus repeated, then shook his head. "They're not here for her, anyway. They're here because the High Priestess—Fade it all, it doesn't matter right now. Or maybe it does. But one thing at a time."

Gus looked between the five intruders to the station, then set his jaw and focused on Chase.

"I'm Gus, Aaron's dad." He offered a hand. Chase raised a brow and crossed his arms.

"She was here first," he stated. Gus raised his brows in surprise, looking through everyone to connect with Ember. She took a page from Devi's book and studied her nail beds, feigning indifference to being treated like an object rather than a person.

What was Chase thinking, drawing attention to her? Some distraction this was turning out to be.

"Everybody come in and let's get this over with." Gus crossed to the hidden gate, holding it open inward so the group could filter through. "Paul, lock up."

Ember's lips thinned and she swallowed her disappointment. Paul not only locked the door, but remained in front of it as she passed. Chase and Aaron lagged, each trying to enforce their right to be the one standing next to her. She twisted to slip past them both and follow Gus' instructions. For now.

"Boys, stay with the Halfer," Gus directed. "Girl, come with me."

Ember's feet stopped between the first pair of desks. A vague warmth radiated behind her and she assumed both Aaron and Chase had flanked her.

"Dad, where are you taking her?" Aaron asked, his voice in her right ear.

"You won't get anything from the Halfers if something happens to her," Chase growled on her left.

Gus spun to glare at the young men, then the 'V' between his eyes softened as he settled a thoughtful gaze onto Ember.

"We're going to the cells." Gus raised a hand as both Aaron and Chase vocalized their arguments. "If your goal is to keep her from the Fae, that's the best space until we finish our business with them. The office is semi-soundproof, but from what I understand, they can deduce plenty just by watching. Should we move this along, or give them more of a show?"

"I'll go with her," Chase insisted.

"You remain here," Gus countered. "Clearly, you two are connected. I won't have you making plans the moment I look away."

Chase leaned over Ember and she shrunk against the intensity radiating off of him.

"I'll stay. I don't want the humans plotting behind my back. But I mean what I say. I can hide my people so well that you'll think we've all fallen off. I will not give you a fading thing if she's hurt."

Ember lowered her gaze, her heart pounding in her chest.

Chase protected her like she was one of his.

With him out there, she could follow along with Gus' plan, whatever it was. He was only partially right that she'd be safe in human cells. That would work until the Fae decided reaching her outweighed preserving the peace.

Gus nodded, but whether it was a promise or evasion was unclear. Shoving trembling fingers into her jean pockets, Ember followed Aaron's dad into the long hallway until they reached a metal door with a small, reinforced glass window in its top third. To the right hung a gray lockbox. Gus entered a code, and with a soft click, the lock released, revealing a row of keys. He slipped one off its hook, then opened the outer, unlocked door, letting Ember in.

A large cell stretched before them, a long metal bench lining the far wall. In the corner, a smaller unit held a forest green cot, its edges neatly tucked. Between the two cells, a frosted glass enclosure divided the space, doors left ajar to reveal small sinks and toilets on either side. The privacy barrier between them stood tall and solid—unforgiving but functional.

The walls were pale concrete, scrubbed to near-sterility, while the dull silver of the bars bore faint scratches and rust specks. Overhead, fluorescent lights hummed softly, their flicker barely noticeable against the stillness. The air held the sharp tang of disinfectant and metal.

At least they were clean.

"We'll put you in the smaller one over here. It's a little more private." Gus spoke as if this was a comfortable guest room instead of a jail.

Ember walked in without saying a word, turning to watch as he closed the door and locked up. When his attention rose from his task to her, his cheeks reddened.

"I'm sorry. Really. Not the way I'd like to do this."

Ember kept her silence.

"How well do you know my kid? Aaron? For how long?"

Ember crossed her arms.

"I'm sure it wasn't hard to win him over. That boy's heart is bigger than this whole town. But I won't have you drag him down with—"

"Stop insulting your son."

Gus's words caught in his throat and he cleared it with a heavy cough.

"How did you get that from—"

"Aaron is the one who tracked me down. Who wouldn't leave me alone. Who constantly reminds me that he thinks it's my fault Brandt has disappeared. Big heart? Perhaps. But don't think there's any room in it for me."

This time, the words caught in Ember's throat, barbed and bitter, as if wrapped in a lie. She refused to take them back. Not after their march into Town. She needed that silly piece of her that had softened toward those puppy dog eyes to believe she wasn't safe with him.

"How often is constant?"

"He comes around for Chase's coffee more than he sees me, if that helps."

Gus peered at the exit as if ready to move through it and past this conversation.

"Yeah, it does." His attention flashed back to her. "I didn't intend —"

"Walking the same line as Aaron, I see."

"What does that mean?"

"You said handling things this way isn't your style?" She gestured to the cage he'd put her in. "Yet here you are, holding the keys in-hand. Words and hopeful intentions fade fast when actions speak louder. So yeah. Just like Aaron."

These charges felt sharper, forged in the smoldering heat of betrayal. Gus studied her intently, as if searching for a crack beneath the surface. Something to help burn through the mystery he was tangled in.

"I can see there's more to unpack than I thought. We'll talk more when the Fae are gone. Let me go take care of that." He hesitated, looking around the jail cell as if he truly regretted having to leave her here. Yet it clearly didn't matter as he walked away, leaving her trapped in the cage.

17

AARON

$\mathcal{A}$aron's eyes followed Gus as he led Ember away, but his focus stayed on her. He silently begged for her to look back and give him even a flicker of acknowledgment, something to express that she wasn't shutting him out completely.

She kept her gaze in front of her the whole time.

"She can take care of herself," Chase spoke.

"What's that supposed to mean?" Paul's fists tightened, and he squared his shoulders. "She's no match for Coach."

Chase raised a brow, an expression similar to one the Halfer had given Aaron at their first meeting. Aaron puffed out a lungful of air, his cheeks ballooning with the force.

"Paul, it's been a trek," Aaron interrupted. "Why don't you and Kyle grab some water or coffee, or a snack?"

"What are you going to do?" Paul asked.

"Hang out here. Wait for Dad. What else?"

Paul watched Aaron for a hard minute, as if he was trying to see past Aaron's simple words.

"I could use a drink," Kyle muttered, hands grazing his pockets. Aaron guessed Kyle was considering something other than coffee, his deep brow suggesting he currently regretted his sobriety.

"Yeah, fine." Paul frowned, noticing Kyle's drop as well. "We'll go to the break room. Need anything?"

"I'm good," Chase spoke. Paul curled his lip but kept his fiery gaze on Aaron, intent on letting Chase know it didn't matter if he wanted something or not. Paul was not there for him.

"No. Thanks. Dad won't be long. If you want to be back…"

"Yeah. Let's go, Kyle."

Paul and Kyle rounded the front desk of the bullpen. When they were halfway to the hallway, Chase tilted his head toward them.

"For the record, Aaron doesn't want this coffee because he likes mine best."

Paul's foot scuffed the carpet, sending him off balance for a step. He flexed, then knotted both hands as he stomped away, Kyle following with less sure steps.

"What in the verge are you doing, Chase?" Aaron demanded.

"I'm figuring out which side you're on."

Aaron's jaw dropped. First Ember doubted him, and now Chase? He mentally collected words, but struggled to form them around the vacuum in his throat.

"Chase. Fades. There shouldn't be any sides. Everyone should—"

"What? Get along? Hold hands and sing songs together?"

"A civil conversation is a good start."

Chase stared at Aaron for a moment before shaking his head and moving past him, sliding off the desk to drop into the spinning chair. Aaron frowned, debating whether to tell the Halfer he wasn't actually allowed to sit there.

"You want everyone to step back and find common ground." Chase said it like it was a bad thing. "The problem is, we don't have that space. Forget what I told your dad. Here's the fading truth. We've already been backed onto the edge of the verge-cursed world. If we go any farther, we'll fall off. There's no fading way we'll give up any of our territory just so they'll be comfortable."

"That's too aggressive. The humans will perceive it as refusing to compromise."

"Well won't that be rich, since all we've ever done is exactly what they wanted. Disappear. And now they want us to dance? Now you want us to dance? No fading way. And frankly, I'm disappointed that you'd even dare to ask."

"Why is everyone forgetting how helpful I've been? I kept secrets. I fought mages."

"Do you assume that's special? We've done those things every verge-cursed day of our lives. You've been here, what? Two months?"

Six weeks, but that certainly wouldn't help his case.

"Will the Fae come?" Aaron perched on the edge of the desk, arms crossed as he worked to change the subject without it being obvious. Chase glared toward the glass office, but Aaron didn't turn to check what the Halfer studied.

"Let's hope not. Did you see their arrows? And Nicu. He's tough to read, no doubt, but if I were betting, I'd say he was there to take her."

Blood rushed from Aaron's face at the memory of Nicu's smooth and controlled violence. He'd been subjected to it himself once, pulled against the larger man's body, an arm squeezed around his throat.

"He protects her."

Chase snorted.

"What gives you the idea that Nicu is anyone's hero?"

"Not anyone. Ember's. He even granted my wish to keep her safe."

Chase's brows rose with that announcement, but Aaron was deep into another memory. This one of Nicu taking the sparks of energy from Ember's hands and letting them drift up to darkened clouds to join with a storm. He'd walked away, then.

Chase shook his head, leaning forward to peer up the hallway. He stood from his chair and rested next to Aaron on the edge of the desk, their shoulders brushing. Aaron cleared his throat and made room. Chase only claimed more space, resuming contact.

"Listen, I appreciate you've had a particular perspective on Nicu, but you don't have the whole picture. Nicu is tied in so many ways to how he needs to protect Ember. How he needs to be loyal to the Fae. You're right, that he can usually be trusted with protecting Ember. But if the Fae Council gets involved… even I haven't figured out how to keep her safe from that."

Aaron blinked, then his eyes widened. "Like learning magic for yourself?"

Chase's scowl deepened, then melted into a half smile. "That might have been part of it."

"So you want peace, too."

"I also want my own dragon, but the odds of that aren't great." Chase combed a hand through his hair in frustration. "Aaron, I know you're still figuring out mages, but Trifecta is nothing new for you. Remember what it was like before you attached yourself to the Trimarked Girl. Recall how you used to spend your time before you started taking on work for the Halfers."

"That's the point. If I can do it, then—"

Chase laughed and shook his head.

"Stop. Just, no. You are not a normal gull, Aaron. Brandt, now, his reaction was more human than yours. If you think about it, you'll see. Look at Paul. Look at Kyle and your dad."

"That doesn't mean it's not possible."

"You're right." Chase's words should have filled Aaron with satisfaction, but the tired, drawn tone of the Halfer's voice kept any elation tampered down. "But will it happen in time? The Fae have Ember in their sights. A few gulls assume they understand her power. Make no mistake, it'll be their version that gets spread around. There isn't a Witch spell on your chest letting you run through a stabbing this time. No Nicu to grant you a wish."

A door opened deeper into the building and Chase refocused on the hallway. Aaron had a direct view of his dad hanging the key back up in the lockbox, closing it with a deep sigh. As Gus passed the break room, Kyle and Paul popped out with steaming mugs, their lips drawn and shoulders tense, as if they'd had their own argument.

Gus's focus drifted between Chase and Aaron's faces to the soft brush of their arms.

"So this is your coffee source," Gus said.

"This guy said Aaron liked his best." The words slipped from Paul's mouth with sharp edges, and Aaron winced.

"Well. Better than I suspected," Gus said under his breath.

Chase straightened his spine, eyes narrowed. "What does that mean?"

"He thought it was Ember," Aaron muttered.

Gus crossed his arms, his lips drawn in between his teeth. Chase didn't soften his posture, but drew in one leg, preparing to stand.

"You mean the Trimarked Girl." Gus spoke, the words thrust from his diaphragm.

"Her name is Ember," Chase countered. He shifted his hip in a motion that appeared lazy, but Aaron wasn't fooled. He was getting ready to jump up if needed. Chase had noted where the key was kept. Whether the lock box would stop a tech-savvy, part-Witch Halfer was yet to be seen.

Gus ignored Chase, not recognizing the same danger Aaron did. Instead, the father focused on his son.

"What have you been doing? What have you been thinking? And for how long?"

"Your son's been trying to gather everyone for a friendly chat," Chase answered before Aaron could. "He doesn't think jailing innocent girls is the way to go."

"She is far from innocent." Kyle's voice was loud, growing toward a shout.

Gus slammed his fist on the empty desk next to him.

"Listen," he snapped. "I have two Fae in there. Do you know why? Because some gnome Priestess died, and now we're supposed to meet and figure out how things will run."

"Dad!" Aaron barked. His fingers wrapped around Chase's shoulder to hold him down as the Halfer's eyes reddened, fixated on Gus.

Gus frowned, shaking his head, eyes wide with warning. "Son. Be careful whose side you take."

Aaron opened his mouth to shout that he supported everyone, but he slapped his teeth together and reformed the words.

"It's not about sides. It's more than that. At the very least, we show respect. Like you taught me."

Gus's brows shot up and his shoulders tilted back as if he needed to catch his balance.

"Our freedom is at stake," Paul interjected. "And not letting these mages keep their fading secrets anymore. That girl, for example —"

"Paul, you don't know what you saw," Aaron interrupted. Paul stepped forward, jabbing his index finger in Aaron's direction.

"Don't you dare gaslight me, Aaron. It sends the signal that you really are taking the mages' sides and are doing their dirty work for them."

"Boys." Gus' firm tone stopped them both in their tracks. The older man had coached them long enough to ingrain obedience from them. "Maybe we should start from the beginning."

"Whose beginning?" Chase murmured, though the humans ignored him.

A soft pop drew everyone's attention to the office, where the door now stood open, held by Janice, the police officer Paul was supposed to ask for the keys to the underground tunnels.

"Gus. Can this wait? We need to finish our conversation with these nice and very patient Fae."

"Yeah. Sorry, Janice." He glowered a warning at the other males. "Everyone just… pick different corners and keep your mouths shut. We'll talk about this when the Fae are gone."

Gus returned to the office and pulled the door sealed behind him. Aaron had watched his movements, but then his eyes caught the dark, scowling features of the Fae.

"Any ideas on why Branna looks particularly pissed today?" Chase kept his question soft, as if she might be able to hear clearly through the semi-soundproof glass.

"I'm not even going to guess," Aaron sighed.

"Verge. Is there a mage you haven't met?" Paul demanded.

"We don't know the guy," Chase offered. He shifted, lounging into the swivel chair with his head resting against the backrest.

Aaron stretched out his neck with closed eyes. At least Chase called them 'we,' though Aaron was nervous that the Halfer might believe Aaron had chosen a side.

Aaron still believed they could turn things around if they could just hold their tempers. He wanted them to recognize each other as people, not enemies.

He only hoped Chase was wrong about not having enough time.

18

EMBER

*E*mber needed less than a minute to survey the cramped cell, including the so-called semi-private bathroom. The steel toilet, stark and unwelcoming, looked more like a punishment than a necessity, while the hip-height basin, cold and dull, barely passed for a sink.

The water closet's frame had been painted darker than the beige on the concrete block wall. A cluster of faint scratches in the metal trim caught Ember's eye, pulling her in longer than necessary. The blocky words, *Kyle's 2nd Home*, cut just deep enough to stand out, followed by a series of hash marks. Likely a tally of how many times he'd ended up in here.

And now he sat out there while she was stuck in his self-proclaimed abode.

Ember let her gaze wander the rest of the room, searching for anything to occupy her thoughts. No other odd markings appeared on the walls or frame—just Kyle's carvings. Either this cell only ever held him, or the other temporary residents were more considerate.

What a pointless mystery to dwell on.

But what else was there to do? Rattle the bars and pretend they might budge?

She sank onto the cot, its thin mattress creaking under her weight, and closed her eyes. How long were they planning to leave her there? Gus mentioned the Fae were here because of Leona, so they were likely meeting due to her death, but why did that matter? The Laws of Convergence were clear: each race lived in their designated section of Trifecta. That didn't depend on who ruled the Coven.

Yet, lately, the humans had been pushing at the boundaries of mage territory. She was in this fading mess because Kyle had gone looking for Brandt, and from what she learned from Paul, he wasn't the only human eager to track down their abandoned children. If the humans were actively searching for the Halfers, these talks might carry more weight than usual. This could go beyond simply adjusting to Leona's absence.

Was this a test? Were the Fae investigating whether the humans might reveal signs of a shift toward aggression?

Ember dug her fingers into the cot, frustration gnawing at her. No matter what was going on with the Fae and the humans, it paled in comparison to her own predicament. Stuck in this cell, her thoughts spun in circles, playing useless mental games while others decided her fate.

A restless itch crawled under her skin. She had never preferred indoor confinement. Being locked in increased her discomfort exponentially. The sterile scent of concrete and faint bleach stung her nose, so far removed from the crisp, earthy air of the forest.

The stillness gnawed at her, burrowing deep into her muscles as an unfamiliar ache. Her lips twitched upward, a bitter smile forming as she realized how strange it was to feel bored with her life hanging in the balance.

The main door creaked open. Ember strode to the front of the cell, straining to see who approached. Were they finally done? How long had it been? Without a clock or windows, keeping track of time was impossible.

Ember's forehead wrinkled when Branna slipped into the

room, letting the door swing closed behind her. Ember checked the Fae's hands for keys, wondering if the girl who'd watched her for most of their lives might break her out. Yet the necromancer's empty fingers hung at her sides in claw-like curls.

"Branna." Ember greeted the Fae cautiously. They were the exact same age, sharing an ominous birthday that had cursed both of them. It wasn't anything they'd bonded over. In fact, mentioning the connection had only made Branna angry.

"Nicu told me."

The vicious bite of Branna's words sent a cold ripple down her spine. Instinctively, she stepped back from the bars. Ember's heart kicked up as she calculated the space between them, ensuring she stood just beyond the necromancer's physical reach.

What could Nicu have disclosed to cause an anger that felt intensely personal? Did Branna care so much about a border breach?

"Did you really think he would keep this from me? I stand at his side—his equal. Not some slip of a hybrid brat who causes more trouble than she's worth."

Branna's words cut deep, her tone brimming with fury and disdain. Ember's chest tightened, but she kept her face neutral, refusing to let Branna see how the venomous insult gnawed at her nerves.

This wasn't about fairness or truth, but power. Branna was staking her claim, asserting her authority over Ember. And if her sharp words weren't enough, the intensity in her gaze, the fire simmering just beneath her calm exterior, made it clear she wanted to scare Ember into submission.

But why now? Ember struggled to piece it together.

Then Branna's lip curled and a small growl pressed through her lips like smoke.

"You let out Edan."

Ember's breath hitched. She stumbled back, bumping into the cot.

"Nicu gave permission." Branna's accusation struck close to the truth. Ember flinched.

Nicu hadn't spoken a word of permission. Rather, he'd walked away at Edan's request, allowing privacy. Space. Letting her keep her secret.

But now Branna knew.

"It was a deal," Ember whispered. "A Fae deal. Edan wanted—"

"I doubt he wanted to die."

Ember's stomach dropped, her knees losing stability. "What?"

"Edan is dead. Because you let him out."

Oh, verge.

Ember bit her tongue, careful not to ask the question pressing up from her gut. *How do you know?* Anyone else wouldn't have. Couldn't have.

But a necromancer could.

That meant Edan's ghost—

Ember's cheeks went cold and her vision blurred.

"Wipe that look off your face," Branna snapped. "You have no right to be sad. To be shocked. You caused this, and I will not let you get away with it."

Ember instinctively stepped back as the shadows at Branna's feet began to spread, spilling across the linoleum floor like spilled ink. They moved unnaturally, cutting stark edges into the light, untouched by the faint glow of the overhead fixture.

Dark fronds rose behind Branna, curling and twisting, their movements unnervingly smooth. Long tendrils stretched through the iron bars, creeping closer to Ember. Her body froze, her breath caught somewhere between her lungs and throat.

Branna's shadows weren't just darkness—they were alive. Their weight pushed through the air, a cold, heavy pressure growing ever closer.

The necromancer didn't move, her gaze sharp and unyielding, but the shadows did. They curled tighter, closer, deliberate in their approach. Ember's legs trembled, but she stayed rooted, torn between the disbelief of this betrayal and the raw terror of those inky streams reaching for her.

This wasn't the Branna she knew, but something darker.

"Branna, I'm sorry."

"Apologies do not bring back the dead."

Ember twisted sharply, trying to avoid the thick tendrils snaking toward her face. The blackness pulsed, alive with cruel intent.

"Nicu." Ember's voice cracked as she grasped at the one name that might pull Branna back from this. Nicu was her guardian, Branna's supposed equal. He wouldn't let this happen, not before he had his chance to control the situation.

But the shadows didn't stop. They lunged forward, slamming Ember into the cold, unyielding wall. She gasped as one thick tendril encircled her throat, pinning her in place.

A sudden blue glow flared across her skin, Ember's own power forming a barrier against the suffocating grip. The energy pushed back, creating a buffer, but it wasn't enough. The coils squeezed harder, forcing her chin upward, cutting off her breath until the need for air overtook her ability to speak.

Ember's chest burned, a desperate gasp clawing its way free. Branna's eyes were darker than the shadows, filled with a hatred that had once been carefully hidden but now flared unchecked.

"Nicu will not be coming to save you. Not this time. I used to think he would always choose you, protect you. But here he is, letting the humans take you. He allowed you to use your power, ignored when you aided the Halfers. Let you open the barrier and let out Edan."

The door sprung wide, banging against the wall as Branna's last words hung in the air like a heavy verdict.

Gus' sharp eyes locked onto Ember. She forced herself to inhale, slow and steady, willing her body to calm despite the residual ache where Branna's shadows had pinned her. The blue glow of her power dissipated just in time, and she stifled a cough, masking her struggle with a slight turn of her head.

Aaron's father didn't flinch, his gaze unwavering. Humans couldn't sense magic, but the tension in the room was thick enough to draw suspicion.

"What's going on here?" Gus demanded.

Branna's eyes snapped to Ember, dark and searing, and then something Ember never suspected happened. The Fae spoke.

"This aberration has allowed a Fae to pass through the barrier."

The words struck like a thunderclap. Ember's lips parted in disbelief, forming the shape of Branna's name, though no sound came. The necromancer's lips pressed together in a tight line, as if she just realized they had an audience.

"You're sure about this?" Gus asked.

Branna didn't reply this time. Her silence was a shield, but the rigid posture of her shoulders only carried her anger, leaving no room for regret.

"I see. Testimony from humans, and a Fae confirming the Trimarked Child can open a passage through the barrier. I suppose that settles it."

Ember swallowed down nausea and sucked in air to combat sudden vertigo.

Everyone was dropping secrets.

How in the fades was she supposed to escape this?

"Dad." Aaron tried to push through the door. Gus held up a hand to stop him, the key to Ember's cell in his thick fingers. "You said you would listen to her."

"Hmph."

Gus walked into the holding room, sparing a glance at Branna's rigid posture.

"If the Fae want to talk to the Trimarked Child, they will

have to wait their turn," he told her. "Your partner has already left. You should catch up."

Branna narrowed her eyes at Gus as if judging his sincerity, or his threat level. With a last glare at Ember, the Fae agreed without words. She exited, taking her shadows with her.

Paul and Aaron made room for her departure, then returned to crowd the door.

Ember sucked in air through her nose, yet it got caught on its way to her lungs. She struggled to judge the expressions on the humans' faces that her brain interpreted as odd geometric shapes with no meaning.

What would Branna do? Wait until Ember came out? Meet up with Nicu, who was likely already watching for her?

No matter that Nicu walked away before; he could not walk away today. His loyalty was to the Fae, just as Branna had so clearly stated.

Yet it wasn't the Fae she faced, but humans. What would their judgment be, now that they knew about her abilities? Would they force her to prove herself immediately? Or would they hold her here until the Fae broke in to retrieve her from this inescapable place?

Gus unlocked the cell and motioned for Ember to step out, his lips pressed into a hard, unreadable line. She hesitated, no longer sure what her next move should be. Maybe it was safer to stay in Kyle's second home.

19

NICU

$\mathcal{N}$icu placed his foot gently onto the forest floor, feeling the sole of his running shoe sink into inches of pine needle ground cover. There was no need for speed here. For once, he had plenty of time.

He did not enjoy it.

Altaya had agreed with Nicu that they needed to follow the humans, though they'd disagreed that Nicu should go along. They split their numbers, sending two of the hunters out to check traps so any game wouldn't be lost to time or other natural predators. That left four Fae not part of Nicu's team engaged in a Trimarked mission.

They were not his only restriction.

Threads of power wrapped around Nicu's organs, deep within where the other Fae could not see. Promise Magic warned him the strands were stretching. Fraying.

Rash decisions weren't Nicu's style, but each slow step forward felt harder than the last. His body held the tension of wanting to be set free, to stretch out and break through the forest with all speed.

Giving in to his body's request for hasty movement might prove to be the wrong choice. With humans involved, his interference may increase the danger. With the Fae following him, their presence certainly would inflame tensions. Then there was the unknown entity of Tristan Glynn.

The space between the massive trunks began to glow faintly, soft forest shadows yielding to the harder edges of human Town. The clean lines of buildings emerged, blocky and abrupt against the natural sweep of the trees. The transition carried an odd scent—damp earth mixing with the faint tang of asphalt and rusting metal.

If it were Saturday, the Fae couldn't have ventured this close without being noticed. But today, the town was quiet, the silence so stark it hummed against Nicu's heightened senses. Yet, at least one of those buildings concealed much more behind their facades.

Seventy-five yards from their position, light glinted off a door as it swung open. Nicu's attention snapped to it, his stride faltering for the briefest moment. Daz stepped onto the street.

The Promise's magic tightened, a psychological snare that translated into a faint constriction in his throat. Nicu swallowed against it, his pulse steady but his thoughts narrowing. Why was Daz alone?

The caution he held so carefully slipped for a moment, but he forced it back. Whatever warning the Promise Magic intended, patience would reveal it in time.

"Signal him," Nicu ordered.

Altaya hesitated only long enough to prove they had doubts about Nicu's plan. Still, they whistled a low note as requested. Daz's movements stiffened, and he stopped, looking around the forest. A moment later, his surprise melted away from his motions and he walked casually in their direction.

No one broke the silence immediately. Nicu split his attention between Daz's approach and the door, knowing he had been paired with Branna.

When Daz spoke, he directed his words toward Altaya, perhaps recognizing Nicu's distraction.

"I take it your presence means you are aware the Trimarked Child is there. Does Center know?"

Altaya paused, as if waiting for Nicu to answer. When he didn't, they filled in the silence.

"We have not appraised Center yet. The Child breached the Fae boundary earlier. We are completing our investigation before reporting."

"Is that why Branna was so pissed?" Daz directed to Nicu.

"This only happened a few hours ago," Nicu answered, intimating that Branna couldn't know because she hadn't been present.

"So you do not have a secret way to communicate?"

Nicu refrained from raising his brow and giving away his surprise at the assumptive question.

"No."

"She has been quiet all day. She did not rise to the bait of the humans and allowed me to handle the conversation. After our meeting ended, she instructed me to leave and she would check in with the Child."

Branna was with Ember.

Nicu's legs trembled, the effort to keep still testing every ounce of his control. He had never struggled to stay in one place before.

Could Branna be the cause of the Promise Magic's warning? The thought clawed at him, unwelcome but insistent. He did not want to believe it, yet she had been the catalyst for the spell's beginning. Fate had a ruthless sense of symmetry; it would be fitting if Branna were tied to its end.

Nicu's eyes burned from holding them open too long, his vision locked on the door Daz had passed through. He breathed deep, expanding his ribs and grounding himself in the moment.

Memory came anyway.

}|{

Nicu paced across the sitting room rug, his feet pressing into the soft fibers, leaving discolored impressions of parallel tracks. Each lap sent restless energy buzzing through his limbs as he practiced quiet steps, judged by whether or not he bothered his suite mate.

He and Branna had shared this apartment for nearly a year, ever since he turned eight. Branna, barely six when she moved in, had seemed too young for the change. Nicu had expected tears or tantrums, certain she would hate leaving the nursery and having her own room. But instead, she had been angry for an entirely different reason.

She despised that their doors faced each other.

The suite had a third bedroom at the back. It provided more visual distance, but she refused to take it because it shared a wall with his.

Now he was stuck in there, trying to make sure he didn't annoy her with his walking practice. Nicu would rather be outside, but the Trimarked Child was at the human school. Though the Fae insisted he watch her as often as possible, he wasn't allowed there. His own lessons finished an hour ago, and so he waited.

Nicu's feet came to an automatic stop when a repetitive knock fell on their outer door. Dropping his gaze to the rug, he frowned at the evidence of his tracking back and forth. He might be getting quieter, but leaving signs behind proved a lack of stealth. With shuffling motions, he scuffed up the path and rushed to the door as a second round of knocking began.

"E-elder Wist."

Nicu's eyes widened for a moment before he brought them under control. He'd missed the chance to stop his words from stumbling over his surprise, but he could at least reset his facial muscles. Wist watched the process with his own impassive features. Once Nicu regained his composure, the Elder stepped inside with an implied invitation.

"I have a new task for you," the Elder stated. "It seems the

Remembrance Spell on the humans is being tested. The Council has decided that the Trimarked Child needs to leave human society altogether."

Wist's voice darkened at the words. Nicu hoped his hard swallow wasn't visible on the outside.

Certainly the Elder wouldn't be asking him to kill the girl. No matter that they hated her, that Nicu and Branna weren't pure Fae, they were still children.

"Acknowledge," Wist demanded.

"Yes, Elder." One answer for both statements.

"You are obedient, and that is good. But I expect your loyalty, Nicu. It is dedication to the Fae and our security that erases the stain of your mutations. Work to keep the Fae safe, to prove your commitment to your kind. The day may come where you will be treated as pure, even if you never truly can be."

Nicu's chest puffed out, and he tried to hide it behind a deep, calming breath. His excitement threatened to bubble up into his muscles, and he worked to smother the tremors.

Wist studied Nicu with a level of scrutiny the young Fae was familiar with. The Elder was his teacher in etiquette and control. Some sessions required Nicu to stand perfectly still for hours, unmoving until the Elder released him, no matter his physical needs.

Since this was not class time, this session only lasted a few minutes. Not even Wist's clothing dared to flare out when he turned to depart.

Once the outer door clicked shut, Branna's door whispered open.

"He is evil."

"He is not." Nicu pinned his gaze on the exit, fearful that the Elder might have heard her.

"Oh, yes," Branna insisted, leaning on her door frame. "I am a necromancer. I know these things."

"Your power is to see the dead, not evil."

"The Fae say it is the same thing."

"It is an aberration. Like being touched by the Trimarked Child's magic." Nicu gestured to himself.

"Not the same! He said you may be accepted. Not me! They will never accept me!"

Branna's shout would have surprised Nicu if it had come from any other Fae, even a seven-year-old. Some Fae wondered if Branna's natural skills blocked her ability to have true Fae control.

"I am sorry." Nicu lowered his chin, recognizing her point while trying to be an example of how Fae should behave. "Evil is just a very big word."

"Four letters," Branna snapped. But a moment later, she offered a small smile. "And fine. He is still not nice."

Nicu didn't have a response to that. In fact, he couldn't name one Fae he'd consider kind in how they treated himself or Branna. Helpful. Teacher. Caretaker. Polite. Which was why Wist was so strict with him, to engineer Nicu's acceptance. To ensure he behaved in a way that allowed the Fae to overlook his mutation. Where the Terraborn were more tolerant, the Gypsum-born Fae were older, harder to convince. Wist would help him do that.

"You can make your own choices, you know. You do not have to be just like Wist." Branna's dark eyes shimmered. Her lip trembled.

As a necromancer, her experience would never match his. But it wasn't his fault she wouldn't get her chance to be accepted, even if she was mad about it. Nicu crossed the living room, stopping three feet away so she wouldn't slam the door before he spoke.

"I will not treat you like they do. I will be greater than Wist. Better at control, and at keeping secrets."

"Better at being mean."

"No."

Branna studied him with an intensity that mirrored Wist's. Nicu stood just as still.

"Promise."

Magic stirred at Branna's request. Nicu retreated from the wisps of power that brushed against his tattoos and short braids.

"That is not allowed."

Branna huffed. "Not Promise Magic. A normal promise that you will not be mean. At least to me."

"That is a hard agreement to make," Nicu spoke slowly. "You thought I was being rude to you yesterday when I sat on the couch."

"I was already there. It was my space."

"It is a big couch. And my point is not that I want to upset you, but what we think is mean can be different."

Branna scowled at him, arms crossed against her narrow frame.

"You think just like a grown-up Fae." Nicu's chest swelled, though he was careful to keep the smile off his face. If he already sounded mature, then surely he was close to acceptance, as Wist had implied.

"Fine," Branna huffed. "No promise, then. But I expect you to be better than Wist, like you said."

Nicu's nod was stronger this time. Proving himself more dedicated than Wist would show the others he wasn't broken because he was an aberration. He would be more Fae than a Council Elder, worthy of honor and respect.

The clock on the mantle chimed, pulling Nicu's attention. It was only noon, but he was tired of being inside.

"Do you want to come today? It is early, so we can walk and arrive at the school on time."

"No." Branna refused as she had every day, eyes narrowed. "I do not want to see the girl who killed me."

They both knew that wasn't what happened, but there was no arguing with Branna. He told her goodbye and left their suite earlier than usual, a coincidence that would align with Ember having been chased from the playground after being bullied off the swing set.

And with talk of Promises at the edge of his thoughts, Nicu freely entered into a Fate-magic forged agreement with Ember Lee, whom he'd found lost in the woods and more alone than Nicu would ever be because he had the Fae.

}|{

Nicu blinked, once, then twice, clearing the haze of memory. No matter how the Promise had started, he had mastered how to bend it, manipulating its intent to keep the frayed edges intact.

His confidence had grown—not just in his abilities, but in his patience. In the belief that Ember understood the limits and would make the right choices.

The door creaked open, and Branna stepped out, her gaze sharp and unreadable. Her appearance offered only surface-level relief. Promise Magic maintained its grip, a coiled presence waiting to snap, and a persistent warning that the day's trials were far from over.

20

EMBER

The interior glass-walled office was somehow worse than the cramped jail cell. It wasn't just the suffocating press of seven bodies crammed into a space meant for half that number. The air carried a filtered, artificial quality, stale and too thin, giving the illusion that it was harder to breathe. The heavy door's secure seal seemed absolute, like a silent proclamation that escape was no longer an option. It reminded her of the End of the World—the jagged road winding down the mountainside, visible but unattainable. Freedom, close enough to see, yet out of reach.

Gus tried to bar Chase from the meeting, but the Halfer threatened to walk out and move the Halfers so deep into the Underground that Gus would have to traverse Tartarus to find them. He'd been allowed inside.

Ember was assigned a seat in front of the bulky wooden desk. Gus and Janice positioned themselves behind it, both opting to remain standing. Chase had grabbed the chair beside Ember, no one else daring to put themselves on her level.

"I won't waste time asking if these accusations are true," Gus began. "How long have you been able to open the barrier?"

"And what will that information get you?" Chase countered. "It isn't like you can go back in time and start killing her."

"We don't want to kill her, we just want out," Paul said.

"I want my son back."

Ember's eyelids fluttered shut, blocking out Kyle's repeated plea—one that would never be answered. Brandt's tragic end rested squarely on Tristan's shoulders. But the humans couldn't know that. And even if they did, the knowledge wouldn't save her. The Wizard wasn't their way out.

"If this turns into a forum, I'll kick you all out. I'm talking to the Trimar—" Gus cut off when Chase leaned forward with fingers steepled.

"To Ember," the older man finished.

Ember opened her eyes, fixing her gaze on Aaron's dad, willing herself to block out the rest of the room. If she shaped the story right, she might get out of this. She had nothing to lose by trying.

"I don't have the control you want me to," Ember answered.

"And it will kill her," Chase repeated.

Paul's voice rose in an unformed vocalization that was cut off with a warning glare from Gus.

"I find that hard to believe, given the evidence that she's done this before and is still sitting here," Janice said, though it was clear Gus held the authority in the room. Ember kept her attention on him.

"The barrier is volatile and raw power," Ember answered. "It nearly killed me once."

"Not to mention that if you arrange a mass human exodus, the mages will absolutely catch on," Chase inserted. "How long do you think you have until they come to get her?"

"We can let the fading mages out too," Kyle muttered. "Surely they'd see the benefit of this plan."

"We are not letting those things out," Paul insisted. "Keep

the magic contained here, trapped and away from everyone else. Who knows what they would do if given the chance to spread?"

"It's possible to leave without them knowing. We just have to act quickly," Janice surmised. "Send large groups at night. Stage an End of the World party and have the cars ready to move."

Ember's chest tightened, her vision flickering at the thought of holding the Veil open for that long. It had taken everything she had to get the six Halfers out today before her strength failed.

"She can only hold it for a few seconds," Chase argued for her. He grabbed the wooden arms of his chair, his knuckles white with effort. "It cuts through anything person-made. It could slam down mid-car and then it won't just be her that you're murdering."

"You seem to understand a lot about this and clearly have experience covering your tracks." Gus planted his hands on the desk and leaned toward Chase. "What would you suggest?"

"Abandon your plan. Let her go. She can keep practicing quietly, and when she's capable of what you need, we'll update you."

"I have family out there." Janice's voice broke, though she refused to look at Ember. "Many of us do. We just want real lives back."

"At the expense of hers."

"It doesn't have to be that way," Gus argued. "Not if we work together."

Ember looked between the faces, all higher than hers, except for Chase, who tried to take the brunt of their attention. It appeared to be working, as they now treated her as a pawn or a tool waiting to be used as they figured out the details.

Details about selecting who would leave Trifecta and when. Who would oversee the process? Who had enough experience with firearms to remain skilled after decades of rationing ammunition?

A grim and bloody future stretched before Ember, where she would become a commodity—protected for her usefulness, not for her survival. Fae arrows would clash against human bullets. Witch magic would slip through cracks, striking human guards. And she would be caught in the center of it all, a power they all sought to control, to claim.

Tristan had warned her about this, explaining that her very existence would ignite a war. She'd dismissed it as another of his manipulations meant to bend her to his will. After all, how could she trust the man who had planted a soul-eating tree and brushed off Charlah's deadly rampage through Trifecta as an "acceptable accident"? Yet here she was, staring down at the reality of his prediction.

"There's no way we'd abandon her in here with the mages after she helps us get out!" Aaron's shout returned Ember to the present, her eyes wide and focused on him.

Of course, he didn't know. The barrier refused to let Ember leave. Even when she opened a passage for others, not so much as a windblown strand of her hair ever passed through. But that detail changed nothing. The room had already devolved back into arguments over theoretical logistics. Ember's gaze flicked to Chase. He focused on steering the conversation into chaos rather than clarity. Her one true ally in this mess.

It wouldn't matter in the end. The humans had uncovered what she was capable of, ensuring she'd never be free again. They'd wring her dry, exploiting her power, and then abandon her to the mages when she was spent. If the mages didn't figure it out first. If they did, it was right back to dark and bloody.

Nicu had always warned her: stay unseen, guard your intent. She had defied him at every turn.

She'd finally gone too far and had run out of options.

"Witches and Fae do not belong in Terra." Tristan's voice whis-

pered at the edges of Ember's thoughts, spilling forward and causing bile to rise in her throat.

She hated her father. She sure as fades didn't trust him. Yet his plan was the only one in Trifecta that felt remotely viable. Return the mages to their home realms and free the humans to theirs. The cost? Feeding the tree. If it worked, maybe it wouldn't just spare her life. It might even grant her the freedom she'd been chasing all along.

Ember scanned the office. The humans had gathered around the desk. Chase stood, his tall frame blocking her from direct view. The main room was empty, but clearly visible. She wouldn't have much time to act and she needed to move faster than the soccer boys and their coach.

Ember slipped from her chair, bowing her back to keep lower than the others' lines of sight. She thickened the Veil magic around her, hoping she had enough strength to break a grip if they tried to reach out. She approached the door without a problem, feeling for the knob, turning it slowly to limit the sound of the latch. The click was quiet. Humans were louder. Ember pushed against the force of the sealed door.

A cool burst of air sped through the opening into the body warmed room. The air pressure popped. Their attention went to Ember's empty chair first, and it was all the hesitation she needed.

Ember bolted. She didn't bother pushing the door closed behind her, knowing speed and her one second head start was all she had.

Fingers brushed her shoulder, and she twisted without breaking stride, her Veil energy working so the person's grip slipped. Too close. She couldn't rely on just running—everyone was faster than her. If she wanted any chance to escape, she needed to be clever and mix strategy with speed.

Ember exhaled, forcing a surge of power into the shield around her body. She sprinted past the desks clustered in the middle and vaulted over the narrow front counter. Smashing into the plastic blinds covering the glass door, she tore back her newly long nails while twisting the lock open. The frame's friction lost her a fraction of a second, but she used her time well. Pale blue energy covered the surface, connecting to every inch of glass. Once through, she slammed it shut, Paul crashing into the door.

Paul pounded on the frame, then put his shoulder into the effort. He launched himself like the bouncer he was. After the impact, his eyes widened, and he stumbled back.

"It's like the End of the World. She made a new barrier."

Gus shoved Paul aside to test the claim. Ember ignored him, her attention caught by Chase. He'd gripped Aaron's upper arm, whispering fiercely into the soccer captain's ear. Then they jogged up the hallway that had led to her jail cell.

There must be a back exit. Chase was on her side, and Aaron was a wild card. Either one might stop her from reaching Tristan, and she couldn't allow that. Ember spun around, racing up the street. All the crossroads here would dead end into the forest. All she needed was to get there. After a lifetime of skirting the edges of Town, Ember could evade the humans much easier among the trees than while in their manicured neighborhoods.

Fifty yards away. Thirty. Twenty.

Pine and mist surged into Ember's senses as she skidded to a halt. Nicu emerged from between the redwoods, Branna at his side. Her shadows dissolved to reveal six more Fae blocking the way forward.

"Stop!"

Two sets of pounding feet closed in from behind. Aaron's voice, sharp and panicked, echoed through the thinning air. To the right, the business district loomed. To the left, a hill of old oaks sloped toward homes blocked off with tall fences.

A sudden breeze cut through the space, warmer than the surrounding chill. Ember's hair whipped against her face, yet the Fae stood unruffled.

Then the world itself seemed to buckle. Ember's chest caved in with a Fate-heavy force, air turning to lead in her lungs. Her body vibrated, every atom pulling away from the next, as if the very fabric of her existence was unraveling.

What was this? Her gaze locked on Nicu. His face remained unreadable, cheekbones etched in shadow, but something flickered in his eyes.

And then she knew.

She'd broken their Promise. She'd left him no choice, and still the sharp weight of his betrayal stung worse than the magic tearing her apart.

Regret tangled with anger, twisting tight inside her. She'd done this, but he had let it happen. Wasn't he supposed to keep the balance? To fight against this? To rescue her from herself at the last minute, as always?

Cold, skeletal fingers clamped around her waist, wrenching her from the ground. Tristan's bony frame pressed against her as he stepped forward, her vision blurring in a rush of force.

Ember's essence snapped back into place, but the relief only underscored the shattered state of her world.

21

NICU

icu and Branna held each other's gaze as she approached. Her return from the human's space was not a quick one. If she'd done anything to Ember, she would have likely been chased out. He would take that small miracle.

When Branna crossed into the forest, he lowered his chin. Let the Fae note it as a greeting, though Branna would notice the slight twitch at the corner of his mouth and the brief flicker in his gaze. Signs of an apology he couldn't voice.

She looked away, and Nicu reclaimed his stoic features. It was her right to reserve forgiveness, no matter how he wished to force it.

"What is going on inside?" Altaya asked. Nicu kept his eyes on the human street, though his ears were tuned to the conversation behind him.

"They are convinced the Trimarked Child is the key to their problems."

Nicu retained the micro-movements of breathing even though no air moved in or out of his lungs. Branna's word choice told him this was about more than the Halfers.

The edges of his vision darkened, and Nicu forced breath

in to cool the inner heat causing the blur. He always knew chaos ruled Ember's choices, and that her human-witch blood would never be balanced by the Fae energy she'd been born into. Discovering that the humans might harbor a secret Nicu had deliberately avoided uncovering frayed the illusion of his patience.

The skin-warmed metal of the Trimarked medallion rested at his nape. His fingers itched to retrieve it, to open the flap and be done. Yet this was only a connection to Ember's power, not to her actions. Right now, with the humans involved, it was a useless tool.

As if his thoughts provided an opening, Wish Magic made its appearance. It sparked in the surrounding air, another force visible only to him. He wondered if Altaya would sense the subtle shift. Hopefully, they mistook it for the same oppressive weight of Promise magic that had shadowed them all day. Nicu held his posture as it thickened and spread out in a murmuration of potential. The last third of Aaron's wish to save Ember could only mean she was in danger.

Seventy-five yards ahead, the glass door burst open, and Ember emerged in a flash of red and black. Her coat flared behind her as long, dark hair caught the breeze. Promise magic loosened its grip around Nicu's neck without releasing entirely.

The surge of Wish Magic pulsed like a heartbeat, underlining the threat to Ember. It wound toward the Trimarked Child as if summoned by her very presence, urging Nicu to ignite the last thread of power tied to Aaron's Wish to save Ember's life.

Yet Nicu held back, certain he could regain control on his own. He did not want the Fae behind him to realize he'd offered a human a Wish while he was still condemned for that long-ago Promise.

Ember spun against the door she'd just opened, blue Veil energy flowing from her body to coat the glass as she slammed it shut. Altaya's breath pulled in low and deep, an echo of how she nocked her bow. A sharp buzz resonated from the Trimarked medallion beneath Nicu's shirt, a reminder that Chaos teetered on the edge of control.

The surrounding Fae moved in practiced unison, weapons rising and arrows at the ready, their calm precision a contrast to the storm building in the air. Each arrow hummed with the faint, foreboding weight of Fate Magic, as it prepared to bring Ember to an unthinkable conclusion.

Ember sprinted up the street, her steps frantic and uncoordinated. She ran blindly, straight into danger.

Wish magic thickened to a near-fog, waiting to be activated, pulsing with passive potential. It pulled in the human whose intentions had shaped it, Chase close by his side.

"Stop!" Aaron shouted, but he commanded no power here.

Nicu clenched his jaw, his fingers twitching as he tried to summon the Promise Magic back to him. He stepped forward, his shoes crunching the forest's edge as he sought to frame the narrative in his mind. Ember hadn't meant to break the Promise. It had been self-defense. Instinct, not intention.

"She has broken her side of the Promise. Let this happen, Nicu." The voice was Altaya's. The words were Wist's.

Promise Magic agreed, rushing toward Ember with an unyielding purpose.

She stumbled, her arms flailing for balance as her breath faltered, her chest heaving with effort as if the air itself had turned against her. Nicu's sternum cramped, a phantom pain echoing her struggle.

No.

The wind shifted, warm and wrong, swirling with an undeniable presence that compounded the danger. Tristan Glynn's image flickered before Nicu's eyes.

"Thank you for this." The Wizard's voice lingered in Nicu's ear, though the Wizard had already moved on.

A sharp sting at the back of his neck drew his touch, where he found only skin.

The Trimark was gone.

Nicu's head jerked up, but it was too late. Ember's form blurred, pulled at a magical speed. In the next breath, she vanished. Only the tattered threads of Fate Magic remained, clawing futilely at the empty space where she had stood.

Altaya and their hunters shifted from watchful to high alert. Aaron and Chase slowed to a stop, their eyes wide as they spun around to search the area.

This was no victory. Fate Magic had not been satisfied and lingered with restless menace, searching for the prey it had been promised. Whispered friction tightened along Nicu's spine, and silent cracks of frayed magic shot pain throughout his body.

"You have failed here," Altaya charged. "She must be found and stopped."

Promise Magic surged with feral intensity, latching onto the hunter's claim as though desperate for any justification to act. It tore into the forest, chasing the faint, fading traces of Tristan's power, but it didn't stop there. The magic refused to release Nicu from its debt, unraveling to coil around his throat. The pressure tasted of raw potential and unrestrained vengeance—freedom clawing for release after a decade of confinement. Both of them had broken their Promise, and Fate's power was hungry for its due.

It wouldn't be satisfied with mere balance; it demanded retribution.

Nicu collapsed under the weight of inevitability. His tattoos burned hot against his skin. Frosted particles of Wish Magic shimmered in the air, swirling into visibility as though even the mundane world couldn't ignore the escalating storm. Dust motes glinted within the magic, beautiful and false—a quiet lie belying the chaos about to erupt.

The Promise lay shattered, irreparable. The cost loomed, demanding payment.

And though it was a tool for miracles, the Wish had not been crafted for him.

Nicu wheezed as he braced himself against the earth. His chest ached, each heartbeat slower than the last, each space between echoing louder in his ears. He gathered the last visage of his strength, calling the visible particles of power to his tattoos, ready to reshape it according to his will.

"What is this?" Altaya hissed.

Branna's sharp, bitter laugh cut the air. "It is his way out."

There were no more options.

This is my failure, he told the Promise.

Let her go.

22

EMBER

$\mathcal{A}$ir flooded into Ember's lungs in painful bursts as her body rediscovered how to breathe. She collapsed onto her hands and knees, each gut-deep inhale rattling against her ribs, and each stuttering exhale trembling through her frame. The ache clung stubbornly, receding far slower than it had invaded her.

She'd escaped the humans—barely. But in her panicked rush, she'd forgotten about the Fae.

They hadn't forgotten her.

Nicu had stood at the front of their line, the shattered remains of their Promise gleaming between them. The weight of her mistakes hit her like a blow, each one an accusation, dropping her to her knees before the pressure fled suddenly and completely.

Tristan. He'd snatched her away, leaving nothing behind but questions that clawed at her already frayed nerves. Why had he helped? What was his endgame? And that magic... would it come back?

Ember's head lowered to the ground as frustration bubbled, roaring through her ravaged chest until it tore free in a scream that echoed through the forest.

"Stupid," she growled through her teeth. She blinked rapidly in anger, refusing to allow the stinging in her eyes.

"I'd call it progress."

Ember twisted, attempting to shift her position, but the effort sent her sprawling. Momentum rolled her onto her back, her hands snapping up in a defensive gesture.

Tristan crouched beside her, his forearms draped over the sharp angles of his bent knees. The trilby hat spun lazily in his fingers while his emerald eyes scrutinized her with an unsettling intensity.

"For example, you did not explode this time."

For all the good it had done her.

Ember let her arms fall to her sides and released the tension from her body. As she lay on her back, she softened against the unforgiving ground. The chill seeped through her jeans, numbing her skin, while her coat offered a meager barrier against the chilled earth. Her breath slowed as she fixated on the patch of blue sky peeking between the wide redwood branches above.

"That looks a lot like giving up."

Ember closed her eyes and breathed deeply through her nose, grateful that her lungs remembered how to perform this very basic skill.

The truth was, she had no idea if she was surrendering. Did she have it in her to get up and fight? Ember's mind was a haze, her entire being stretched far past its limits. Yet her heart still beat out a persistent rhythm that didn't feel like quitting.

Ember moved one body part at a time to assess the damage. Her fingers twitched, her toes curled, and her chest heaved as each breath came smoother than the last. She bent her knees, the heels of her sneakers scraping against the ground as her muscles protested the motion. Her thighs acted as an anchor as she wrapped numb hands around them and pulled herself upright. The effort left her trembling, her arms weak, but she forced herself to sit, refusing to focus on the cold ache spreading through her limbs.

Tristan stood a few paces away, silent and still. He made no move to assist, whether from indifference or cold calculation, leaving her to wrestle with her exhaustion alone. Perhaps he was waiting for the perfect opportunity to strike.

There was really only one reason he'd rescue her, after all. Though Ember had nearly convinced herself to work with him while escaping the humans, a deep part of her screamed that helping Tristan would lead to nothing good.

Ember anticipated the moment the Wizard would lay out his carefully organized thoughts and request, once again, that she lend him her power. Yet all he did was watch her catch her breath while she tested her ability to move.

She was well-versed in silence, but this quiet, unbroken observation from Tristan was different. It crept under her skin, setting her nerves alight and sending goosebumps rippling along her arms. She resisted the urge to shift or glance away, determined to hide how much it rattled her.

When he finally broke the silence, his voice was low and measured, carrying a weight that caught her off guard.

"I know what it's like when a world falls apart."

"I'm fine."

Tristan ignored her lie.

"To have your place in the order of things erased."

Ember's eyes narrowed. "You've been here long enough to realize I don't have a place to lose."

"Oh, but that's not true at all, Ember dear." Tristan stopped spinning his hat. "In fact, when I returned, I found you far more connected to this society than I had dreamed possible when I left seventeen years ago. Caring for your mother. A key partner of the Halfers. Able to walk freely onto Witch soil and having dedicated, if tense, Fae guardians. I'm sure you're not surprised to realize I had hoped you were thoroughly cut out of all societies. It would have been so much easier to gain your help if you'd known the truth from the beginning."

"Which of your alleged truths would that be? That the Trifectans aren't to be trusted? Well, neither are you."

"That you are meant to be used, Ember Lee. The Halfers have been smart about it, offering you a trade. As you learned today, the humans won't be so generous. As for the Fae, they'd rather see you destroyed than have anyone access your power."

Tristan's voice was flat, filled with a logic that lacked sympathy. He wasn't trying to comfort her or even warn her. He was laying out the facts so that his solution appeared as the best one.

Perhaps it was.

Nicu had officially chosen the Fae.

She'd always hoped he'd choose her. Ember had collected memories as evidence to prove he might. In those moments he didn't show up while she practiced her power. Those times he walked away before their conversation drew too close to the truth. When he told her that intention mattered more than actions.

Were those lies, or had her mind twisted reality to fit what she needed to believe? What was he doing now? Regrouping? On his way already, able to follow Tristan's trail even if he couldn't match the Wizard's speed?

How long had she taken to recover?

Ember pushed herself to her knees, her palms brushing against the uneven, rocky ground littered with dry pine needles. The rough surface bit into her skin, grounding her as her eyes darted upward. Shafts of pale winter sunlight filtered through the towering redwoods, their branches creating jagged patterns of light and shadow that danced across the grey expanse of granite around her. In some places, the stone glittered faintly, patches of milky quartz flickered like fractured stars.

"We're on Witch lands," Tristan offered freely. "As far from the human Town as possible."

"Why?"

"To be safe from the wretched Fae, of course. They can't come here without permission, and the grieving Coven is still recovering within the confines of their ruins."

"No," Ember snapped. She had already figured out that part. "Why did you save me? And don't say it's because I'm your daughter."

"That's not a wrong answer, though you are correct that it's not the whole reason. As I've said before, your power is necessary. My preference is for you to agree to aid me."

Something hid beneath those slick words, something Ember could sense, but not grasp. She wasn't surprised he kept something from her. The question was, did it matter?

Did she help him or face the Fae?

Did the humans force her to use her power, or did she willingly assist Tristan with his plan?

He was so fading logical. So incredibly tranquil. After today, the choice should be easy. But.

"I don't trust you."

"You don't have to," Tristan assured her, his voice calm, almost disarming. "You just have to trust them less."

'Them' being everyone else. The Fae, the humans, Nicu— all of them had failed her in their own ways.

Her fingers flexed, her body frozen between distrust and self-preservation. The Promise Magic had made its stance clear. No one would save her, not really. She had to choose.

Ember swallowed hard and forced her voice to steady. "What do I need to do?"

Tristan lifted his hat, momentarily obscuring his expression. He wasn't quick enough to conceal the fading edge of his crooked smile, but with a smooth motion, he adjusted the trilby atop his head, masking any trace of emotion.

"First, we stand up." He offered her a hand. She ignored it

and climbed to her feet. Tristan unfolded his body, sharp angles unbending into unforgiving straight lines. He reached into his coat and pulled something from an inner pocket.

"And then you use this."

Ember's breath caught as she stumbled back, the uneven ground shifting beneath her.

Dangling from Tristan's fingers was a medallion. A pentacle intricately bound to a butterfly wing on the right, with delicate chains swaying from the lower tips.

An exact, physical copy of the Binding Ink etched onto the nape of her neck.

The Trimark.

23

AARON

aron's legs locked beneath him, the world spinning into slow motion as Ember vanished before his eyes. His breath caught as Nicu crumpled to his knees, his dark skin tinted an unnatural purple hue, then he fell face-first into the dirt.

"Get them," Chase barked, yanking Aaron by the sleeve and shoving him back up the street. The force jolted Aaron into motion away from the Fae, while Chase used the opposing momentum to launch himself toward Nicu.

Aaron glanced over his shoulder, his heart hammering as Gus and Paul sprinted to close the distance, though there was no sign of Kyle or Janice. Ember's shield must have failed.

His knees buckled with indecision. He wanted to go to his dad, but his feet refused to move, his mind unable to reconcile the sight of Nicu sprawled on the ground.

How? Why?

Gus reached Aaron in a few long strides, his grip firm as he caught Paul mid-surge, keeping him from following Chase. The tension in his father's jaw meant he held back his emotion-fueled words. There would be a conversation about trust and honesty later. But one crisis at a time.

"We need to find out what they did with the Trimarked girl," Paul shouted, trying to yank his arm from Gus' grip.

"You didn't see?" Aaron asked.

"That bitch's magic kept us in there until she was gone," Paul spat.

"Aaron, what happened?"

Father and son shared a tense glance before their eyes shifted to the unmoving Fae. Chase ignored the arrows as he fell to his knees at Nicu's side.

"Ember vanished, and Nicu—he collapsed."

Paul stopped struggling against Gus. His breath sucked in as his gaze fixed on the fallen figure.

"Wait. Is that her Fae guardian?"

Aaron nodded. "And he's the strongest person I know. Nothing attacked him. Ember just disappeared, and then he fell."

"The girl escaped." Gus's brows shot up, refocused on the Fae and their weapons. His lips pursed in thought, as if he ran plays in his mind and figured out there was no way Ember outran the Fae. "How?"

Aaron let out a lost huff, shrugging his shoulders. One of the Fae had stepped closer to Chase, their arrow pulled taut despite the short distance between its point and Chase's exposed neck. The Halfer never stopped touching Nicu, his fingers feeling for a pulse, a breath, and looking for signs of injury.

"Magic is invisible to humans," Aaron offered.

"So she has more skills than just keeping us locked in here." Paul's voice had lowered in volume and octave. Aaron's lips thinned and he shook his head.

"She can't do anything like that."

"So was it the Fae?" Gus asked.

"Look at them." Aaron's hand shot out as he gestured toward the group at the edge of the trees. The Fae stood their ground. Branna watched from the back, fingers against her deep frown. The hunters' arrows were drawn and aimed at Chase, but their wide eyes focused on Nicu.

"Fae are immortal, or close enough," Gus murmured. "They just saw one of theirs fall and don't know what to do. If they had the Trimarked Child… Is this all of them, or are more in the area?"

"That's impossible to tell," Aaron answered. "But the only person who disappeared was Ember. It was as if she—"

Aaron closed his eyes on memories of being trapped in his own head, his body dragged around at the Witch Queen's command. Within her hive mind, he glimpsed things he shouldn't know, including how the Wizard Tristan could manipulate space and time to move at speeds no eye could track.

"There are other mages who want Ember. It might be one of them."

Aaron's shoulders curled forward and his chin dropped. Gus stepped closer, his brow furrowed.

"She was ours first." Paul at least had enough sense to keep his volume down. "She has to pay for keeping us in here. She has to get us out."

Aaron straightened and faced his old captain. When Paul graduated, the mantle passed to Aaron. Not because his dad was Coach, but because he'd put in the work and earned it.

"Stop," Aaron snapped. Paul's skin reddened, his expression caught between disbelief and fury, but Aaron didn't flinch. "Do you even realize why she kept this a secret? And don't you dare say it's to trap us. It's because of what happened back there, in the police station. The second you found out, you decided to use her, no matter what it cost her. You ignored everything she tried to tell you because you refuse to believe the truth. What you want from her? It will. Kill. Her."

Aaron vibrated with restrained rage. Gus' hand landed on his shoulder, but Aaron shrugged it off as if it weighed nothing.

"And humans aren't the biggest threat," Aaron continued,

his voice gaining a gravely texture. "Humans can only use their voices. Mages are capable of much worse."

Paul's face twisted, his brow furrowing so deeply, it cast a shadow over his eyes. He spat his response like venom.

"What in the realms, Aaron? Do you even care about freedom? Or have you really become such a mage lover that you can't see she's lying?"

Aaron's fist flew before his brain caught up. Pain exploded in his knuckles as Paul staggered, clutching his face.

"Fall off," Aaron swore.

Paul wiped his mouth, his sneer returning as blood smeared across his skin. "Gladly. Once I get ahold of your pet."

Aaron surged forward, but Gus stopped his charge, locking an arm around his chest.

"Let him go." Gus' voice was firm, his grip unrelenting. Aaron's chest heaved as Paul walked away.

"I'm not chasing him. There are more important things."

Aaron turned his back on Town to hurry toward Chase. Gus grasped Aaron's shoulder, tightening his hold as Aaron tried to escape.

"Stop it," his dad ordered. "You've been acting strange all day. I know you. I want to support you, but I don't understand what's going on. Why are you more worked up over the mages and that girl than Paul? Brandt, even."

Aaron swallowed the anger trying to claw its way up his throat. He was sick of people deciding for him who or what mattered. In fact, he wanted nothing more than to skip this conversation, but Gus wasn't relenting.

"It's not important right now."

"Your friends aren't important." Gus threw his hands in the air as if giving up. The frustrated tilt of his brow turned away from Aaron, like his dad needed a break from his incomprehensible teen.

That was it.

"Of course they are! All of them. Even those!" Aaron punched his finger toward Chase and Nicu. Gus blinked, then wiped a palm down his face.

"Aaron, I warned you. No."

"Don't you dare say that." Aaron trembled, the ache in his throat hot and raw. "You taught me respect. Teamwork."

"Yeah. With your team. Not the other guys." Gus's voice cracked, his eyes widening as he held out his hands, silently pleading for his son to understand. "We only win the game if we're focused on us."

Aaron blinked rapidly. He couldn't take being told he was wrong again, especially by his dad.

"There's a way." Aaron cleared his throat, willing his tone to steady. "There's a way to fix this."

"Not without losing people who care about you."

Aaron's gut clenched as the words hit harder than a punch. Life as a Halfer flashed through his mind. Having to leave his cozy home, drop out of school. Scatter whenever a human came around, because none of them could be trusted with the Underground's secrets.

"Y-you?" Aaron's stomach twisted, his voice barely a whisper.

Gus's cheeks flushed, eyes wide and arms limp at his sides. He shook off the reaction, then stepped toe-to-toe with Aaron.

"Don't be stupid. Never."

A shattered breath rattled through Aaron's chest, his whole body trembling with the constant shots of adrenaline. He dragged a shaky hand through his hair.

"Then trust me," he said, his voice gaining strength. "We need to be over there."

Gus raised wary eyes to the group of Fae, his brow wrinkled, lips pursed.

"Back on the pitch, then."

Aaron didn't wait for further permission, and he ran toward Chase. His dad followed and their movements brought

Fae attention. Two of the archers shifted their aim from the Halfer to the humans. Gus stopped in his tracks at the show of force, but Aaron took his cue from Chase and knelt next to Nicu.

"Is he dead?" Aaron whispered, not able to believe that this impervious man was gone.

"Almost," Chase murmured. "But not yet. We can work with that."

"He needs to get back to Center," the Fae at the forefront spoke.

Chase ground his teeth. "We have been over this. He'll die if you move him."

"He will die anyway." The Fae's even tone startled Aaron, his jaw dropping at the lack of emotion in the mage.

"You don't care?" he asked.

"The aberration made his choice." This time, a film of venom coated the words. What had Nicu done to deserve that hostility?

Aaron searched for Branna, finding her standing slightly apart from the others. Her features were also impassive, but the shadows at her feet flickered and writhed, stretching outward in hesitant bursts before retracting.

"Branna?"

With Aaron's inquiry, her eyes snapped to him, then to Gus, who approached slowly, as no one had shot him yet. With a final frown directed at Nicu's body, the necromancer pivoted abruptly and strode away.

"What the fades?" Aaron wheezed. "I thought they were—"

"It's complicated," Chase interrupted. "Now get me a leaf, or a dead butterfly, or anything else lightweight."

Aaron looked around desperately, but only saw pine needles and concrete. The trees on the street had already lost their leaves and been cleaned up for compost.

"Will paper work?" Gus asked.

Chase's neck twisted so quickly, Aaron winced for him. "Yes."

Gus dug into his pocket and pulled out a palm-sized notepad. He tore a sheet off and handed it to Chase.

"Just one?"

Chase nodded and reached toward the ground where he'd discarded a small velvet bag Aaron recognized from the night Chase had healed his leg wound. He picked out a light blue milky stone Aaron didn't recognize, along with a jagged piece of amethyst. He caged the crystals in one hand with three fingers, then held the slip of paper between the remaining two.

"Devi, get here right now!"

His lips moved faster, the sounds slipping beyond the range of human hearing. Aaron recognized the signs of a spell being cast. The note twitched as if alive, struggling against the grip constraining it. When Chase released it, an unseen breeze snatched it up, spinning it into a white blur that vanished into the air.

"You have already called her," the Fae leader mocked. "I suspect your Witch has no interest in helping a Fae."

Chase ground his teeth and Aaron placed a calming touch on his shoulder. This Fae didn't understand. They hadn't been there when Ember was swallowed by magic. They didn't know how Nicu and Devi worked together to find the Trimarked girl. How each of them confronted the danger of the Witch Queen in their own way.

"What is going on?" Gus' voice lost the deep tones of his Coach persona. Aaron looked at his father, surprised to recognize uncertainty wrinkling the skin surrounding his eyes. His powerful hands hovered in the air, accustomed to action but unsure where they belonged.

"Power surged around Nicu after Ember left." Chase seemed to accept Gus without question, particularly after his help with the paper spell. The Halfer returned his fingers to the pulse in Nicu's neck as he spoke, ensuring the Fae was still alive. "Fades. It's slower."

"The power surge?" Aaron asked softly.

"Right. Visible magic! It's fading impossible. Did you see it?"

"I was dealing with Paul," Aaron muttered.

Chase shrugged as if the answer didn't matter. "Maybe you were too far away, but who knows? Like I said. Unheard of. It started when Tristan took Ember."

"Tristan?" Aaron demanded, looking around the forest as if he could somehow catch sight of the slimy Wizard.

"Who is that?" Gus asked.

"One of the other mages who wants to use Ember," Aaron answered. "This isn't good. He's her father."

"Her father isn't good." Gus repeated words as if he'd captured them just to check if he truly understood their meaning.

"It's a long story," Aaron replied with a sigh.

"Seems like there are a lot of stories I've missed."

Aaron flinched at the soft tones of Gus' voice. He usually only sounded like that when they spoke of Aaron's mom.

"Dad, I'm sorry."

Gus raised a hand. "We'll do that later. For now, what about this guy? A brace? Some kind of medicine? We have a generic kit at the police station —"

"As if something human could help this."

All Fae arrows shifted, abandoning their targets to hone in on the presence that materialized along the forest path. Loose cranberry curls framed the face of a wild, curvy Witch, her mint-green eyes gleaming like polished gems. A fur-lined berry parka ended at her knees, revealing the edge of a bright yellow wool skirt that swayed with each step.

Devi had arrived, but it wasn't with the blazing energy Aaron expected from her. Would that work in their favor?

Her gaze dropped to Nicu, and a frown pulled at her full lips.

"Or Fae magic," she murmured, feeling the air before her. Devi stopped inches from Nicu, jerking her hand back. "Or Witch."

Chase shifted from his squat to a seated position on the ground, his movements slow and heavy as the color drained from his cheeks.

"No," Aaron said, his voice cracking under the weight of disbelief. "You're wrong."

"I told you before, human, do not think you understand everything about magic just because you've spent a few days with us." Devi's retort was softened by her deep distraction.

Gus's shoulders tensed, his discomfort evident at the disparaging tone Devi used with Aaron. His lips pressed into a thin line, but to Aaron's relief, he stayed silent. Aaron's mind raced, too tangled in his own spiraling thoughts to manage both the mages and keeping Gus from stepping into dangerous territory with the Witch.

"But you know how to help him." Aaron's voice teetered between a command and a plea, weighted with urgency he couldn't hide.

Chase slumped forward, head in his hands, missing the shift in Devi's expression. She lifted her sparkling eyes to meet Aaron's desperate gaze. Amusement softened her features, a faint pink brushing her cheeks as her lips curved in an arrogant, knowing smile.

"Of course."

24

EMBER

"What is that?" Ember curled her lip at the dangling Trimark. The dark silver medallion absorbed light like a black hole, its energy radiating an unsettling, menacing pull. She recoiled instinctively, her stomach tightening in protest.

Getting close to it felt unthinkable. Touching it was out of the question. And yet, Tristan expected her to wield it?

"What does it do?" she asked, her voice thick with distaste.

"If I'd known a little trinket would prompt you to start asking the right questions, I would have shown it to you ages ago."

"You've always had that?" Ember's breath caught in her chest. She took another step back, not bothering to fight against the understandable tremors vibrating through her limbs.

"I've possessed it for a short time, but I've known where it was for a while. Your dedicated Fae guardian has been carrying it around under his braids."

Ember's stomach dropped toward her feet. Nicu had this? Why? What did it mean?

"I don't want it."

Tristan caught the amulet in his fist, then tucked it away.

"I can see we have a discussion ahead of us. But for now," Tristan extended his empty hand. Ember stared at it as if it were just as dangerous as the medallion he'd pocketed.

"Would you prefer I carry you to No Man's?"

Oh. He wanted to leave.

But leaving meant she'd have to use that talisman. Ember took another step back.

"Hmm." Tristan lowered his arm and studied her. "What are you experiencing right now? And be exact. I need to understand why this small piece of jewelry affects you so negatively."

"I don't like it." Ember's words tumbled out as if they were practiced. "It's dangerous. Not meant for me. I don't want to be anywhere near it."

"Oh, but Ember, this medallion was created specifically for you."

Ember snorted. "Not likely."

"I'm completely correct about this," Tristan insisted. "I helped design it."

Ember froze, her eyes focused on Tristan's face as if his features would somehow tell her if he was telling the truth.

"I didn't make it, of course. This is pure Fae artistry. But I did help with the planning."

"You… But you were gone when I was born." Tristan remained silent, as if he saw the gears in Ember's brain turning and wanted to give her time to put the pieces together. "So you knew before… They knew before? But they tried to kill me!"

"Ah. They did not, in fact, have all the information. Regrettable that they tried to end you, and thankfully, fatefully, avoided."

Another connection clicked into place.

"You are working with the Fae?"

"Only when strictly necessary." Tristan spoke through his teeth, nose turned up at the very thought. "In my haste, I'm sure I didn't explain things fully. Thankfully, they figured it out in time to bind you."

"The binding didn't work." Ember shook her head. "You know that."

Tristan's smile was slow and sharp.

"Oh, Ember. You have no idea how effective it's been." He patted his pocket. "And this here is the key. Don't you want to experience what you're fully capable of? To learn what you were made for?"

A chill ran down Ember's spine.

"You have a way of making me regret agreeing to help you."

"Well, then. Let's get going before this tenuous truce falls apart, shall we?"

Tristan didn't wait for permission this time. He gripped her around her upper arm even as he opened a path and led them through Witch lands. When they reached the edge of No Man's Land, he let go and Ember stumbled against the sudden loss of momentum.

Outside the triangular clearing, Tristan stood tall, his warm gaze focused on the tree he'd grown from souls.

Disgusting. The thing he adored killed people, for fade's sake.

Yet, here she was, helping it grow by getting ready to feed it with her power.

"No more hesitating," Tristan warned in response to her involuntary step away. "It only takes the Fae about twenty minutes to run this far. It's been fifteen."

Ember glanced at the sky, finding the sun much lower than she'd suspected and marking the late afternoon. They remained on Witch land, yet were still vulnerable if the Fae or humans appeared.

Ember assumed they'd stopped outside the dead zone because Tristan's trail couldn't pass the boundary. From what she understood, this area was barren because it lacked all magic. While magical energies thrived in the Fae and Witch realms, even human lands held traces of it within the molecules of living things. Humans simply couldn't access it.

"Let's try this again." Tristan reached into his pocket and pulled out the Trimarked medallion. Ember recoiled.

"I understand you want nothing to do with this, but please recognize your reaction for the Fae trick that it is. Of course they spelled this device to be abhorrent to you. They don't want you to claim it. Will you let them win?"

Ember thought of Fae arrows. Fae rules. Fae deals.

Fae Promises. Fae betrayal.

It made sense that the Fae would take measures to keep her from something that increased her power.

No matter his ambitions, Tristan wouldn't hurt her. Not when he needed her.

Ember swallowed hard, trying to repress the revulsion growing in her gut. She stepped closer to Tristan, though her hands remained on her thighs, fingers tapping in a subconscious rhythm.

Less than a minute later, she stood inches from Tristan and the medallion. Another thirty seconds passed before she managed to raise her hand toward the trinket, with each second dragging as if it spanned a week.

With each movement closer, a heavy refusal burdened her, as if a force field held her back. Ember clenched her teeth against the sickening cramps in her lower abdomen and closed her eyes, convinced this was magic. The Fae trying to control her once again.

They'd subdued her for too long.

Ember's eyes snapped open. She reached forward erratically, her fingertips brushing the metal. With a quick grab, the edges of the butterfly wing were digging into her palm.

The pressure faded. The nausea in her gut eased. Ember uncurled her fingers, lips parted as she took in a deep breath.

So this is what her tattoo looked like. Her mother and Devi

had explained it to her, and she'd glimpsed it as best she could with paired-up mirrors, but seeing it in metal form was something different.

It was beautiful.

The butterfly wing was far more complex than she'd imagined, its inner wing an elegant lace. Tiny chains trailed onto her wrist, tickling softly. Thinner than expected, the pentacle star was crafted from fine wire. Her breath hitched as she stared at the intricate design. Awe rippled through her chest, mingling with a gnawing bitterness that spread through her ribs. Something so small, so delicate, had defined the boundaries of her life, limiting her in ways she couldn't fully articulate.

Yet, unlike her tattoo, the upright star on the medallion lacked the angled line that cut through its center.

"Why isn't it broken?" Ember asked, her voice barely above a whisper, her thumb tracing the edges.

"A pentacle is employed when calling and harnessing power, a tool for mastery over magic. Your tattoo is crossed out to strip you of that control. The medallion you hold can remove that block, not that the Fae ever intended for its use. Magic, you see, follows certain rules. The binding spell they cast needed an anchor, and in this case, they used that little trinket."

The emblem felt heavier than its size should allow, as if it carried the weight of all the choices she hadn't been allowed to make. How much of herself had been caged by this thing—an object she'd never even known existed until now?

Ember shifted her attention from the Trimark to the Wizard. "What do I do?"

Tristan closed his eyes and drew a deep breath, tilting his face toward the sky. The shifting branches overhead let dappled light play across his features, casting him as divine one moment and demonic the next.

"I just need to savor this. I've been waiting twenty years for it. More, if you count the time during the Fade where I tried to stop it."

"You said the Fae could arrive soon."

Still, Tristan took his minute. When he finished, he pointed at the tree.

"You will take the Trimark to a spot where energy flows freely from the cave. Stand there, and then connect to the tree."

Tristan faced her, one palm hovering just below hers, as though offering unseen support to the medallion she held aloft.

"There is a small clasp on the outer wing," he instructed. "The butterfly body is a clever hinge. When the wings open, they'll frame the pentacle. Your power will unlock and be awakened. That's what you feed into the tree."

"So simple?" Ember asked with a frown.

"As with everything, this isn't as easy as it sounds. Recall being trapped in the Veil energy. Think of the power that flooded you."

A shiver ran through Ember's body and she shook her head.

"I don't want to do that."

"It won't be the same." Tristan's tone sharpened, and he inhaled through his nose. "This is not the Veil. You are merely a conduit, Ember. A catalyst for greater things. This is the reason you exist."

"To feed a tree?"

"To break the barrier and open the door so mages can return home. And they must go home."

Ember looked between the medallion and the fibrous bark of the sequoia, a deep frown on her lips.

"And you'll be here to help?"

"I will ensure everything goes as it should."

Not entirely comforting. At least Tristan needed her alive for this.

"To echo your earlier rebuke, it has been a while since I

took you from Town." Tristan's quiet reminder sent Ember's attention out toward the forest.

"Are they close?"

"Not yet." Still, the warning was enough. The Fae would come. How much longer would Ember stand here deciding?

Even knowing she didn't have time on her side, Ember couldn't force her feet to move faster than one step per full breath. She approached the sequoia on trembling legs, studying its exposed roots and low branches to see if it would reach for her as it had done in the cave below. For now, it remained stoic and tall, just like any other tree around them.

Ember circled the massive base, her steps deliberate as she searched for the flow of energy Tristan had described. Her skepticism gnawed at her resolve—she was more human than mage, after all. Would she even sense the magic he spoke of? The bark under her fingertips was rough and ancient, its grooves wide enough to swallow her fingers.

Just as she opened her mouth to ask for help, a faint tickle brushed against the sole of her foot, spiraling upward along her shins like an electric whisper. She froze mid-step, her breath catching as the sensation bloomed into something deeper— subtle but undeniable. She located Tristan, who had kept pace with her, though on the outside of No Man's.

Why wasn't he coming inside?

"Good. You found it. Open the medallion." His spindly fingers flared along with his words, his eyes wide and fixed on her every move. She appreciated his attention, yet a big part of her wished he watched for Fae instead.

Moving forward was the only way to escape them now. Ember examined the wings of the Trimark as Tristan called out further instructions.

"Once the energy flow starts, you must press the medallion into the bark. It contains a Fae signature, so the tree needs to absorb it before the power vacuum in this space can break."

Her left hand pressed gingerly against the deeply grooved

bark of the sequoia, its texture fibrous and slightly giving beneath her fingertips. The ridges seemed to bite into her skin as if reluctant to let go. She flicked open the medallion's clasp, its delicate chains quivering in her grip.

A sharp, high-pitched screech tore through the air, piercing her ears like the scream of metal against metal, and Ember jumped.

"Just a bird," Tristan called, his words fast and breathy.

Another shaky nod, and Ember found the seam between the wings. With trembling fingers, she eased the hinge open. The butterfly wing folded outward, settling alongside the left pentacle, a perfect match for the one on the right.

Ember's chin flew up as the tingle in her feet became a wild rush through her body. Her joints flooded, the tissue expanding to the edge of tearing. Blue power burned from the depths of her bones and surged into her blood. The two energies mixed in a fluid tornado, pressing up and out, releasing through the palm of her left hand.

Above her, the sequoia came alive. Its towering branches stretched outward, defying borders as they spread across the divide of No Man's. The trunk climbed upward, shoving against her arm and forcing her elbow to bend. She tried to lift her leg, but her feet were caught in swelling roots. Her ribs heaved as fear clawed its way into her throat. Was the tree going to swallow her where she stood?

"The medallion!" Tristan's voice cut through the rising storm in her mind. "Feed it to the tree!"

Ember's fist clenched around the pentacle, its butterfly wings sticking out from the sides of her grip. She gritted her teeth, trying to force her arm upward, but her body wouldn't obey. The energies converging from the cave below and the Veil within her had turned her into a prisoner in her own skin.

Her vision blurred as her strength faltered. Her right hand refused to move. She couldn't give the Trimark to the tree.

So the tree was coming for her instead.

25

DEVI

*D*evi staggered out of the magical path, her first attempt at crafting one. The landing was far from graceful, her hand slamming against the rough bark of a nearby tree as if to steady her swirling thoughts. Wide mint-green eyes scanned the scene before her, disbelief twisting into irritation.

Four Fae stood in a tight formation, their bows slung low but their postures rigid. Nicu lay crumpled, his face slack. Chase and that infuriating Aaron knelt by Nicu, acting like nursemaids while an unknown human stood over them. The absurdity of it left her reeling. Nicu, of all Fae, out cold. And where in the verge was Ember, the center of the disaster Chase had been flooding her with messages about?

Devi pushed off the tree, her heart heavy even as her sharp mind took over. She didn't want to be here. She wanted to go back to her solitary study, admittedly hiding from painful realities. But this was the price of knowing too much and caring just enough.

"Devi, Ember was taken by the humans and the Fae are pissed at her, too. I'm going to follow Ember. I have a feeling we'll need you soon."

Chase's first voice message had arrived clinging to a dried, brittle leaf. It hadn't enticed Devi from her hidden cove: a snug, secluded cave tucked into the cliffs bordering the Circle. The dragonling had led her there, and she had no intention of leaving until the Coven elected their new High One.

She dove back into her work, the comfort of experimentation creating a shield between her and the real world. The dragon bone ring sat before her, its spellwork a complex weave of shimmering threads. Devi leaned over it, her fingers brushing the edge of her notes, tracking the intricate pattern of the magic. The deeper she studied, the more the thread paths became clear, each new line revealing its secrets.

This looked familiar.

A second note, this time written on a deeply veined maple leaf, dried to a dark, dirty orange and unmistakably from Town. *"Devi, the situation just got worse. We officially need you."*

A surge of heat coiled in Devi's core, rising like acid to burn through her chest. It wasn't her job to mediate between the Fae and humans. Nicu would handle it. He'd swoop in, save the Trimarked girl, and all would return to the usual chaos.

Devi crushed the brittle leaf in her fingers, the crackle sharp in the still air. Tiny flecks of debris clung to her skin, and she wiped them off against the rough edge of the stone, her movements brisk and final.

She took a few deep breaths before returning to her notes, reclaiming her thought process, then reaching for a second notebook. Flipping through the pages, she folded it open on the best representation she'd been able to piece together for the structural patterns of Ember's Binding Ink tattoo. After studying it for a moment, she flipped over to Nicu's Living Ink, then back to Ember's.

The Inks and the dragon bone ring spells shared a similar structure. The magic had the same skeleton, though they belonged to different things. Devi's spine lengthened and her cheeks flushed. She rested the Ink and ring patterns side by side to identify where the Works overlapped.

The matching pieces were subsections of their unique spells, like side trails off a main road. They attached to the primary function, but then separated in order to…

"Devi, get here right now!"

Devi snapped upright, yanked from her concentration as Chase's message screamed at her. The scrap of paper hovered inches from her face, its words desperate and loud, reverberating in her skull before she even touched it. Her fingers curled into fists, nails biting into her palms, as red frustration blurred the edges of her vision.

The dragonling pressed closer, its massive taloned foot resting gently on the open notebooks, blocking her path back to her work. A silent but firm instruction.

"Fine." The word ripped from her throat, raw and rasping. "Fine. Fine. Fine!"

Every movement was stiff with anger as she stuffed her materials into her messenger bag, shoving the books and loose pages in with less care than they deserved. She placed her gear deep within the cove's shelter, ensuring it was out of reach. The dragonling twisted in a slow circle before settling down protectively over her belongings, a low rumble signaling its readiness to guard.

Devi glanced at the creature, her emotions too tangled to form words. All she managed was a curt nod before turning sharply, leaving the cove and her irritation behind.

As she navigated the narrow goat trail to the forest floor, she turned her brain from one problem to another. She calculated that her fastest way into town would be to reconstruct the spell Tristan used to move through the realm. But Devi hadn't cast it before.

The idea of trying something new burned off the last

threads of irritation with a burst of intellectual adrenalin. Once off the trail, Devi pressed up the fur-lined sleeves of her berry-colored parka. She focused on the layered bracelets circling her wrists, each adorned with precious gems. Bound in webs of hemp string, the stones were held securely until she chose to release them.

Tourmaline for a speed boost and safety along the way. Garnet to supply energy, and the creative focus would help her shape this new spell work. Black obsidian for grounding, clarity, and protection. And citrine to support bending space and time, and to clear the path.

Devi cradled the four gems in her palm, then locked them into her fist. Closing her eyes, she pulled magic from the stone and air around her, filtering the raw energy through the gaps between her fingers and shaping it with the crystalline structures to let the power blend within her grasp.

She imagined her route, one that avoided boulders, trees, and other pitfalls. Where taking a single step carried her the distance of a mile. With carefully practiced motions, Devi rolled the gems until they suspended between her fingers, then thrust her hand before her, palm out. The magic wound between the crystals like a tapestry until it bound together to cut her path.

A smile crept across her face as she paused to test the Work, ensuring its stability before committing to its use. Flawless.

One step blurred the world around her, and she fought against a sudden wave of motion sickness. Two steps later, she swallowed hard, her stomach twisting in protest. Quickening her pace, she managed three more strides before stumbling to a halt, the path ending abruptly at the sight of Nicu lying face-down on the ground.

Her spell needed adjustments, but that could wait. The scene before her demanded her attention. Ignoring the Fae's granite-tipped arrows aimed her way, she moved toward Nicu. Their silent threats held no weight; the long-standing agreements between their people ensured the Fae wouldn't dare harm her.

Devi knelt between Nicu and the Fae hunters, her sharp focus cutting through the chaos. Chase and Aaron huddled on the opposite side of Nicu's prone form, their bodies tense, thighs pressed together as if bracing against the weight of their anxiety. Their frantic energy pulsed in the surrounding air, but Devi didn't absorb it. Her world narrowed to the immediate problem before her. A fallen Fae, his life teetering at the edge of a delicate balance.

"He fell after Ember disappeared. I don't know why. First she couldn't breathe, then he couldn't brea—" Aaron's words came quick and blended. Devi stole his air for just long enough to stop his rambling.

"Shh. Roll him onto his back," she ordered. Aaron hurried to do as she asked, a tight cough accompanying his movements. Devi reached a hand toward her half-brother. "Chase, give me your clear quartz."

Chase searched in his velvet bag until he found a quartz wand the length of her thumb. Chase wasn't allowed bracelets, so he made do with a pouch of mis-matched stones, which worked in Devi's favor for the moment. She captured the threads of the spell fragment surrounding Nicu, then expanded the crystal to study the patterns. The Fae edged back slightly, their discomfort with Witch magic evident, though they refused to retreat entirely.

"Why is she staring into space?" the older human asked. He leaned over Chase and Aaron, as if closing the physical distance might enhance his ability to understand.

"It's magic." Aaron watched Devi, one hand absently rubbing his chest. "We can't see it."

Devi's gaze darted over the tattered threads of magic, her

stomach sinking as her brain made sense of the mess before her.

This wasn't a spell—at least, not anymore. The web of energy had been shattered, its broken edges jagged and cruel, now embedded in Nicu's vital organs like barbed hooks, slowly siphoning his life force.

"Stupid Fae. You broke your Promise."

"The Trimarked Child broke it first. That Fate attacked him can only mean he was complicit. He made this choice." The voice came from behind her. Devi didn't bother turning to see which Fae had spoken, but assumed they were their leader.

The sentiment shared was inaccurate, anyway. The Fae clearly didn't know how long Nicu had been playing this game. This spell should have broken years ago. That it hadn't been was testimony to the sheer strength of Nicu's will.

But why did he let it break now?

Not such a difficult question to answer with the array of Fae behind her. He'd never been able to pick a side.

Fading Fae. How dare he be so reckless, threatening to take away his stoic presence and more of Devi's stability with it? She'd already lost the cornerstone piece of her life and struggled with the rubble. Losing someone else could shift the broken pieces and leave her drowning in them.

"How long?" Chase asked.

Devi shelved the useless emotions. They would not help her here. She parted her lips to warn that Nicu had mere minutes left, but snapped them shut when the realization struck. Chase wasn't asking how much time Nicu had. He was asking how long it would take her to fix it.

Could she fix this?

Why not? Wasn't she the most powerful Witch in generations?

The spent Promise Magic was useless now. Devi dismissed the remnants of the spell and reset the crystal. With steady hands, she brushed it against Nicu's tattoos, ignoring the sharp hiss from the Fae behind her. The crystalline projection of Nicu's Ink flared open before her. The first time she'd encountered this intricate web, its complexity had left her utterly lost. But after studying it alongside the dragon bone ring, she had gained a deeper understanding of its structure, enough to pinpoint precisely what she needed.

Devi traced the Veil line with precision, her focus narrowing as it twisted and knotted into a distinct node. With a flick of her fingers, she expanded the intricate knot, and a sharp grin split her face at the revelation.

Ember.

They were tied together, likely since the moment Ember was born. The chaotic web of events suddenly made sense. A Fae spell had attempted to destroy Ember, but her Veil energy had deflected the attack. Nicu, caught in the crossfire, had been young enough for his molecules to absorb the massive influx of power. Branna's death and Nicu's desperate use of Ember's inner energy to bring her back were the final threads binding them all.

Curious that Branna wasn't directly tied into this magic. She'd be connected somehow, but Devi didn't have time to untangle that mystery right now.

"All your black and white stones," Devi demanded of Chase. She'd need incredible protection for what she was going to attempt next. "Arrange them on Nicu's chest."

Chase placed the gems as requested. Devi grunted as she worked to pull the sticky Terran magic from the ground beneath her and the closest tree. The unrefined energy resisted, clinging stubbornly to the earth, but she wrestled it free with sharp bursts of focus, channeling it into the stones.

Devi envisioned a protective shell forming around Nicu, a buffer to shield the physical world from the volatile energy she was about to manipulate. The gems pulsed faintly in her palm, growing warm as she aligned the power with her intent. Once the spell stabilized, she propelled it into his tattoos, targeting the intricate pathways connected to the Veil. Her focus sharpened on the node that linked Nicu and Ember, funneling the magic into the shared connection with a precision that left no room for error. She needed to tap into the raw, molten power without it reaching back out and burning her to a crisp.

Devi's Work struck true. Veil energy resonated with a hum that sent faint ripples through the node. Blue light flared, illuminating the tangled threads of the spell with a soft glow. Devi guided the power to weave itself into something restorative. Each shift was deliberate, precise, reshaping the chaotic remnants of magic into a pattern that could heal rather than harm.

Nicu's muscles spasmed, his body reacting to the influx of stabilized energy. His chest heaved in a long, drawn breath, breaking the unnatural stillness. The rise and fall of his breathing evened out, steady and rhythmic, a clear sign the magic was taking hold.

It was working.

Then the Veil node pulsed. Flashed. Erupted.

A flood of raging power surged through the connection from Ember's side, sweeping away all of Devi's careful work in an instant. The ground beneath them shifted, a subtle but unrelenting quake. The air spiraled upward, carrying grit and dust that stung Devi's eyes.

Devi pulled back, the elemental strength of the Veil crashing against her. It was overwhelming, untamed, and she redirected all her energy into her personal shielding. She didn't have Ember or Nicu's protections to safeguard her from its ferocity.

The shared node flared violently, exploding with a blinding, lightless energy that erased all her senses. Devi cried out, thrown backward by the sheer intensity. Her hands slammed against the ground, scraping stone as she scrambled to keep her head from hitting the dirt. She blinked furiously to clear her vision.

Through the haze of ringing silence and residual magic, she searched desperately for Nicu's form. The protective shield she'd built was shattered, rilled with pulsing wisps of pale blue energy. Devi's stomach twisted, cold and hollow. She staggered to her feet, trembling with the unfamiliar weight of irrevocable failure.

Nicu was gone.

26

EMBER

"*Tristan!*"

Ember pulled against the sequoia's bark. Her left hand stuck fast as the tree grew around it. The roots beneath her feet swelled and shifted, locking her legs in place. "Get me out!"

"Give the tree the medallion!"

Her father's growl sliced through her panic, his voice raw with urgency. Ember flinched, her breath hitching as she tried to turn her head. But she couldn't. Her face stayed locked upward, the weight of invisible forces holding her rigid. Only her eyes moved, darting to the edge of her vision where Tristan's silhouette hovered at the border of her awareness.

"I cannot move!"

Tristan dipped his chin, letting the brim of his hat cast a shadow over his features. With a slow shrug, he dropped his arms, his long coat sliding off his shoulders and pooling on the ground. Beneath it, his vest caught the light. A striking emerald green at the center, the silky fabric was flanked by a kaleidoscope of small, glittering gems that had been hidden until now. As Tristan lifted his head, the crystals shimmered, their glow intensifying without touch. The colors swirled together, creating a milky radiance that pulsed in rhythm with her frantic heartbeat.

"What are you doing?" Ember jerked harder at her arm, wincing at the strain in her shoulder joint.

"There's one thing I neglected to mention when I explained your purpose." Tristan's gem-like eyes gleamed, reflecting the magic coursing through his spell. "Your willing participation allows for a cleaner connection. Less wasted energy, you see. But your power is also uniquely suited to be controlled by any mage who knows what he's doing."

A rigid stiffness overcame Ember, locking her muscles and overriding her desperate attempts to escape the ever-expanding tree. Her bones ignited with searing heat as the magic from below surged through her body like a wildfire. What had seemed a strong current before was nothing but a trickle compared to the raging torrent now consuming her.

Tristan had seized control. That's why he was outside No Man's, so he could play this trump card. He latched onto her power as Devi had done in the caves, as he himself had attempted when they first met. This time, he didn't falter at her cries. He funneled her magic relentlessly, using her like one of his crystals, feeding the sequoia without regard for the way its swelling trunk crept ever closer to swallowing her whole. No Man's Land flooded with the power of the cave, the magics of all realms rising to meet Tristan's call.

"Give it the medallion." His teeth cut off the sound between each word, making his meaning more than clear. "It can't break through without it."

Ember focused past the tree's massive branches, eyes straining toward the sky. The sequoia matched the height of the surrounding redwoods, its upper limbs bending against an invisible dome. The redwoods pierced through the barrier effortlessly, their tops swaying freely above it, but the sequoia was trapped, just like everything else in Trifecta.

And Tristan wanted her power to change that.

The scorching pain gnawing at her body threatened to scatter her thoughts, but Ember fought through it, dragging forward every reason she'd agreed to this. The mages needed to go home. Susan deserved a life free of magic and the constant fear of what it might do to her daughter next.

But was this agony justified by the cost? Was surrendering her power to Tristan worth gaining freedom from all the others who sought to do the same?

Her trembling fingers squeezed the medallion. All she had to do was press her hand to the tree and let it absorb the Fae artifact as Tristan commanded.

Ember focused on her right arm, willing it to move. It refused, stiff and unyielding as if the Trimark itself were fighting her, its weight magnifying the crushing force of the power locking her in place. Could it be resisting the tree on its own, adding its defiance to the overwhelming pressure that held her immobile?

A shadow fell over her. Tristan pressed against her back, his imposing frame towering over her. His breath was hot against her ear as his hand closed firmly around her clenched fist, trapping the Trimark in her grasp.

"Enough of this."

With Tristan's added strength, her body gave way, and he forced the medallion toward the tree. Ember cried out, her elbow twisting as if tendons tore under the pressure. The deeply grooved bark of the sequoia bit into the backs of her fingers, its rough ridges scraping away layers of skin.

"Let it go, little Ember."

Ember fought to release her grip on the metal, but searing pain radiated throughout her arm, each wave dragging her closer to unconsciousness. Darkness edged into her vision, blending with the relentless burn of magic coursing through her veins.

"I can't," she gasped, each word punctuated by the sting of fresh sweat sliding down her skin.

"Then the tree can take you."

"No!" Her shout cracked, raw with desperation, but Tristan didn't even flinch. He forced her hand against the swelling trunk, his strength unrelenting.

The sequoia surged forward, its bark creeping over her knuckles. Through the haze of pain and betrayal, Ember's gaze darted to her father. He stood still, unmoving, watching as if this was the plan all along.

For a fraction of a second, Ember wondered if this was the right ending anyway. To have this tree swallow the Trimark in all its forms: medallion, tattoo, and girl.

For fade's sake.

It wasn't a thought worth entertaining. She was done with use without control. It was time to set her intentions.

She was screwed either way.

Ember clenched her jaw and drew in a steadying breath through her nose. The flow of power already burned, and she was still cooperating. When she started fighting back, it would only get worse.

Don't think about it.

She inhaled deeply, once, twice. Three quick breaths followed, desperate attempts to brace herself.

Her eyes squeezed shut, teeth grinding as she fought to summon the strength to harness her power. It wasn't enough to want control. She had to find it, had to push past the searing pain that threatened to shatter her resolve.

As she struggled, the sequoia's trunk swelled higher, its bark curling outward. It reached for the medallion, and for the first time, it tasted the tang of Fae metal.

The barrier fractured.

Ember screamed, the sound raw and guttural as agony ripped through her. She'd experienced this before. There'd been a sharp, slicing pain along her spine when Tristan had cut his way into Trifecta. But this? This was worse.

Every new rupture in the Veil's fabric echoed across her

skin as if she were the barrier itself. Her nerves burned, each one alight with searing fire, and her blood roared in her ears, pounding with the force of an unrelenting storm. It wasn't just pain—it was an invasion, her body a battleground for magic far beyond her control.

She'd survived being swallowed by the barrier.

She'd fought off the Witch Queen.

She'd protected her friends.

She could damn well protect herself.

Ember tore her power free from the Wizard's grasp, claiming it as her own despite the agony tearing through her. Energy erupted from her like a shockwave with a force that sent him stumbling.

Gritting her teeth, Ember seized control of her limbs, her trembling hands steadying as she lowered her chin. Her gaze locked onto the sequoia, its branches writhing as if alive, the air surrounding it heavy with its insatiable hunger.

Refocusing the power flowing through her, Ember redirected it into the shield coating her skin. It flared into place until the moment it hit the tree. Ember pushed against its resistance, keeping her intention on the energy she controlled, struggling to slip between herself and the enveloping wood.

Small cracks whispered toward her, this time from bark breaking. Space eased open around her hands, though the medallion stuck. Once her fingers could twitch, Ember redoubled her shield on her left palm and pressed it against the trunk to use its counter pressure to pull her right hand out.

Without the connection to Fae metal, the tree's strength faded. Ember's movements were stiff but her own as she freed her legs, then staggered a few steps away from both the tree and the Wizard. Tristan reached for her, but her shield flared, forcing his fingers to slide off harmlessly. A relieved gasp escaped her lips as she released the torrent of magic that had been pulled from the cave's depths.

Her chest heaving, Ember spun to face Tristan, her eyes

wide open in more ways than one. The world around them remained eerily unchanged, save for the tree's towering height, its expanding girth, and the delicate fractures spreading through the barrier above. The maelstrom had been inside her and nowhere else.

She'd made a mistake. Obviously. Tristan might have the answers on paper, but the truth was far more hidden.

He'd been willing to sacrifice her. The determined set to his thinned lips told her he still was. She kept her feet firmly in No Man's, knowing it was her best bet at the moment since he couldn't use his magic while he stood in this space. Outside of here, there would be no getting away from a Wizard who moved as fast as lighting.

Which clearly meant she would have to fight.

27

NICU

*V*ibrations rippled through Nicu's awareness. Sound teased at the edges of his perception, sharp and dissonant, each note pricking like tiny needles against his senses. A faint, electric burn coiled through him, a sure sign of Veil magic.

"You are the most reckless of beings." Altaya's voice sounded muffled, as if spoken through several layers of cloth. Nicu strained to move, to force his eyes open, but the effort met a wall of nothingness. His body felt distant, unreachable. A memory instead of something solid.

"You don't understand," Devi panted. "That power was not mine."

Of course it wasn't. Only one person in Trifecta had control over the barrier. Nicu willed himself to rise, to find his feet and chase after the wayward Trimarked Child, to uncover the chaos she'd undoubtedly set loose.

The effort splintered into a burst of static, crackling through the nothingness surrounding him.

He didn't have a body to command. He was nothing more than raw energy, a fragment of existence barely held together. But if Promise Magic had already exacted its price, why was he still here? Why hadn't he been erased entirely, scattered into oblivion?

His question brought instant awareness to the Veil energy that pierced through the realms of the living, the dead, and the odd in-between Nicu found himself. In the physical world, new cracks in the barrier etched into his soul.

Then his perception shifted, leading him to the source of the damage. No Man's Land loomed in his consciousness, a scene out of Fae nightmares. Ember's energy spiked, but not by her will. Tristan controlled the rush of power through her delicate form, forcing it into contact with the wide-open Trimark medallion trapped between her fist as the tree slowly swallowed them both.

This was what he'd left behind. This was what he'd failed to stop.

Fate Magic was right to take him.

No.

Ember wasn't the threat. Tristan was. Nicu needed to return, to protect Ember and the Fae by ending the Wizard's schemes once and for all.

Called by his need to save Ember, untapped Wish Magic sparked against the edges of his sightless consciousness. Nicu coaxed it closer, drawing it into the fragile boundaries of the energies holding him together. Let it recognize the tether he still had to Ember. The wish hadn't been intended for him, but he was Fae — born to bend the threads of fate to his will. Aaron had been careless with his wording, and Nicu was prepared to exploit every ounce of its potential.

I am her guardian. Chosen on the day of her birth. I am the only one who can keep her safe.

Wish Magic expanded, sifting through his fragmented intentions before faltering. There wasn't enough of him left to guide its flow. If he fully dissolved, the magic would scatter entirely, leaving Ember to fight on her own.

Though he failed to command the Wish, his efforts

summoned the full force of the universe upon him. From beyond, a razor-thin strand of Fate shot in, embedding itself deep within the fragile threads connecting him to the world of the living. Chaos energy encircled what remained of Nicu like a sharp-toothed trap.

This was not right. He had planned carefully. Practiced patience. Maintained stability. Perfected control.

A wave of inevitability surged through him, pressing down like a physical weight on his being. A silent insistence that the balance would tip, no matter how fiercely he resisted.

The impression wasn't his own. Fate and Chaos anchored him in their grip. Their presence was undeniable, their unyielding hold a testament to the price they had come to collect. His chest tightened—not with fear, but with wary calculation. He had fought their influence at every turn, but now, face-to-face with their will, he tread carefully against their claim.

At nine years old, Nicu had believed self-control was enough to balance his duties. He protected Ember by isolating her. He safeguarded the Fae by keeping the world at bay. And he remained with his people by standing on the outskirts.

But the distance hadn't been sufficient. Chaos had slipped through the cracks, embracing Ember like a long-lost daughter.

Now it claimed him too, entwined with Fate, holding him in this half-life and forcing him to witness how Ember was being used to tear Trifecta apart.

Nicu's vibrations softened, his remaining consciousness blurring as the universe's judgment pressed against him. Responsibility wrapped tight around his neck like an unrelenting chain. Chaos and Fate weren't offering a boon. They were delivering a sentence.

In death, he was forsworn.

Agony ripped through him, tenfold, as if to strip him of the last pieces of himself. But Nicu refused to unravel. He gripped onto the final threads of his essence, holding firm.

If he was still there, he had a chance at redemption. The universe wouldn't waste energy keeping him bound if it didn't believe he had a purpose left to fulfill. He opened up his mind, expressing a willingness to accept their message.

A flash of shattering iron bars, jagged and broken, rippled through Nicu. Chaos's exhilaration licked at his senses, wild and unrestrained. The shards scattered outward, each a streak of brilliance slicing through the dark expanse. Within the apparent disorder, an underlying structure emerged. Chaos's unpredictable energy being guided by Fate's unseen hand. Like the roots of an ancient tree, steady and unyielding, the fragments aligned with a purpose, converging toward an inescapable truth.

Harmony over Balance. Flexibility within Order.

Ember faded into the heart of the vision. Her power surged in vivid threads of blue and gold, twisting in an intricate dance. Swirling energy enveloped her in a Venn diagram of danger. Interaction with Fae forces, and the realm fell apart. Engaging with Tristan's flowing Witch magic, and the same devastation unfolded. Amid the turmoil, there was a flicker, a faint thread that tethered Nicu's essence to Ember, and remained resolute against the storm of destruction.

Purpose coursed through him, steady yet laced with an unsettling shadow. This mission was the one he'd been shaped for, forged and reforged from the moment he'd used Ember's power to save Branna as a child.

He could protect the realms from Ember's untamed potential and shield her from her personal brand of chaos. Convincing the Fae of her necessity would require precision and restraint. He would need to temper their anger, weave a compelling argument, and make them see she was indispensable to their survival.

It would be no small task, but his entire life had been spent navigating the impossible. This was another precarious balance, and he was determined to maintain it.

The weight of the universe crushed the thoughts in his mind, stopping him from piecing together a plan. The impression slammed into him like a hammer. Nicu, on the line between Fae and Ember, his attention torn and time flying past him. Ember slipping toward destruction, taking that small chance at peace with her.

You must choose.

The universe hummed with restless energy, holding him fast in this in-between state. Nicu struggled against the pull, his thoughts a fractured storm. The Fae came to mind. Their mistrust, their rigid devotion to order. Then Ember, her fire and chaos barely restrained, her power capable of igniting the realms.

You empowered them both, and now the world is at stake.

Aaron's wish. Ember's recklessness. The Fae's unyielding position. Each one, a thread in the same tangled knot, and he was ensnared at its core. Images crashed through him, laden with the unbearable weight of the gravest consequence: all realms on the brink of destruction.

This soul-deep manipulation was why the Fae resisted Fate and Chaos and their demands to have a single, inescapable path. For eons, the Fae had faced these forces with unyielding defiance, marked by the rise of the Ternate Star, their vigilance guarding against Chaos' attempts to drag them back onto Fate's gilded track. All rooted in their unwavering belief. There was always more than one way forward.

To return, you must choose.

A stalemate. Nicu loathed the weight of it, the inevitability pressing against him like the edge of a blade. Yet he knew it could not hold forever. He would have to act, to choose. But he was Fae—adept at sidestepping the binds of Fate and Chaos, skilled at weaving truth into threads they couldn't sever. He needed only to find the right words, the precise balance to tilt the scales without losing himself.

I will do what is necessary to save the realms.

The universal forces stilled, heavy with scrutiny. They pressed into the core of his existence, weighing his thoughts and resolve, testing the sincerity of his pledge against the relentless flow of time.

Acceptance.

The frayed threads of Aaron's Wish converged, strengthened by Fate and Nicu's unwavering belief that he alone could save Ember. Drawing on the last remnants of the Fate Magic, Nicu's essence reassembled, a reverse unmaking that solidified spirit into muscle and bone, tethered by the inked marks etched into his skin. His braids reformed against his scalp, their weight familiar. Clothes draped over his frame, rough fabric settling into place as if conjured by the memory of their texture.

Gravity pulled him down, and Nicu dropped from the nether with a silent grace. He bent a knee to absorb the impact, his landing muted against the scorched earth. Around him, pine needles had been reduced to smudges of ash, the ground scarred by the aftermath of chaotic energy. The acrid tang of burned resin lingered in the air, and the stillness of the redwoods pressed against his senses.

"What the fading verge, Nicu!" Aaron's shriek cut through the tense silence, stopping Altaya and Devi's conversation cold.

Nicu straightened, scanning the edge of the forest where the trees met the pavement. The lingering hum of disrupted magic buzzed at the back of his mind. He'd returned. But the fight was far from over.

"What happened to you?"

Though Altaya's voice was soft, Nicu caught the faint quiver beneath their words. He followed their gaze to the backs of his hands, where long, irregular scars etched lines across his dark skin, stark against the even darker tattoos.

With deliberate movements, he pushed up the sleeves of his coat and sweater, revealing that the jagged marks continued up his arms, branching like the veins of lightning.

So Fate and Chaos had felt the need to brand him.

"The price for not dying," he offered simply. One of the costs.

"Huh." Devi stepped closer even as the others backed away. The path of the Witch's gaze suggested his new scars climbed his neck as well. "They almost resemble a child's clumsy attempt to piece you back together."

Close enough.

Heat radiated from the blue marks, and he fought against a wince. He raised his attention to the upper dome, expecting to find the space crisscrossed with breaks that mirrored his pain. Yet the magic remained invisible and all he saw was a bleak, cloud-laden sky.

The damage must be limited, then.

Nicu recalled the vision of Ember's hand swallowed by the ever-growing sequoia. The blue marks on his skin pulsed with the pressure to comply, to make his choice. He kept frustration from showing on his features, though lack of expression wouldn't fool the Power monitoring his thoughts.

Yes, he had agreed to the deal. But he would do this his way.

Without a word, Nicu surged forward, his steps sure and steady, as if the nether had never unmade him. The Fae fell into formation behind him, their movements synchronized and silent. A shimmer of magic tore through the air, and in a blink, Devi appeared at his side, her measured strides contrasting his all-out sprint.

He didn't stop them. Let them come. The end deserved an audience.

28

EMBER

The stillness of No Man's Land enveloped Ember, daring her to mistake its silence for safety.

In this space of rot, no birds chirped their afternoon songs. The wind skirted the triangular clearing as if repelled by its very existence. At its center, Tristan's tree towered, an unnatural monument to survival, its roots gorging on the magical energy of the cave below.

Death permeated both places, though. Here, Brandt had died. Below, Leona had lost her life.

The way Tristan glared at Ember, she might be next.

"You disappoint me, Ember."

"It will build character."

Tristan's lips pulled away from his teeth in a sharp snarl.

"Why don't you understand? You must cooperate. You know the risks, so there's no point in wasting my breath. The work here demands sacrifice."

"You mean I should stand by idly as that thing tries to swallow me." Ember's hands balled into fists at her sides, nails biting into her palms.

"If you had followed instructions—no, never mind." Tristan waved a hand dismissively, his tone sharp. "I should have known better. You were created to be controlled. A walking, breathing source of power crammed into a little girl's body. Without someone to properly manage you, any success you achieve will be nothing more than a lucky accident."

Tristan approached Ember, his footsteps deliberate, each one a declaration of pretension. Instinctively, she shifted a foot back, raising her hands in a defensive stance before her mind registered the motion.

"Cute," he said, the word dripping with disdain.

The Wizard's spindly fingers snaked around her right wrist, the pressure sharp and commanding. Ember's grip faltered under his hold, the medallion slipping from her grasp. It fell into his waiting palm, the soft clink of metal a cruel punctuation to her momentary defeat.

"Time to correct our course," Tristan said, his gaze fixed on the Trimark, ignoring her entirely. He gripped the delicate butterfly wings with both hands, their intricate edges catching the light. With a calculated twist of his wrists, the hinges snapped clean from the pentagram, the sound brittle and final.

Ember's neck ignited in searing pain, as though the tattoo etched into her skin was being ripped away. She choked on a scream that refused to form.

A pulse of raw Veil energy surged from her chest, violent and unrestrained. The force hit Tristan, sending him stumbling back, and billowed skyward in a blinding wave. The sequoia trembled, its upper branches drooping and curling in response. Ember's power slammed against the Trifectan barrier, rippling across its surface in brilliant waves. The cracks the tree had labored to create were smoothed over, sealing with sharp precision.

"In all the hells of all the realms!" Tristan bellowed, his voice cutting through the charged air like a blade. Though the Veil's blast had sent him sprawling, he wasn't defeated. He scrambled across the ground with the determination of a predator closing in on its prey.

Ember spun on her heel, heart pounding, her instincts screaming for her to run. But Tristan was faster. His long fingers tangled in her hair at the base of her neck, yanking her head back and her body with it.

Tristan yelped, jerking his hand away as transparent blue flames licked along his skin. He slapped at his palm, then frantically patted his pant legs, extinguishing the ethereal fire with quick, panicked movements.

Ember collapsed to her knees, unsteady as the sudden release of pressure threw her off balance. Scattered tufts of black hair fluttered to the ground, and her fingers instinctively reached for the back of her neck. Heat met her touch, the uneven ends of her hair seared and jagged. She jerked her hand away, hissing softly at the sting.

A cool draft swept against the newly revealed skin, raising a shiver along her spine. Goosebumps prickled her shoulders as the truth settled in. For the first time in fourteen years, her tattoo lay bare, exposed for all to see.

"What the verge is happening?" Ember gasped, staring at several long strands of hair tangled around her fingers.

"Accidents," Tristan extended the sound of the word until it hissed through his teeth. "But one that can be corrected."

Ember struggled to stand, her legs trembling and unsteady from the power's explosive release. She slipped, collapsing to the ground, but quickly flipped onto her back, keeping her gaze locked on Tristan. She refused to let him catch her off guard again.

Golden and dark yellow gems embedded in Tristan's vest ignited, their light sharp and vivid as if drawn from the heart of a flame. Magic pulsed to life, flowing through the intricate network of stones. Tristan worked with precision, his fingers weaving the power into a tangible, glowing rope. With a flick of his wrist, he sent the spell lashing toward Ember.

A sapphire-blue shield erupted around her, crackling with raw energy. Ember gasped, scrambling backward in a desperate attempt to widen the space between them. Her palms slipped against the dirt as she pushed with her heels kicking up loose soil in her haste.

Tristan didn't move. His focus remained sharp, his predatory gaze locked on her. The rope of his magic twisted and writhed, moving with unnerving intelligence as it advanced. It slithered toward her shield, testing its boundaries with relentless determination.

"Trimarked. Stop!"

Ember concentrated on the Wizard's spell, though she was keenly aware he was no longer the only threat. It was one of the Fae who spoke. They had finally arrived.

Was it in time, or far too late?

Was she only trading one danger for another?

Her pulse thundered in her ears, but she couldn't afford to follow the Fae's command to stop. If she did, Tristan's magic would bind her. His intent was unmistakable, etched in the cold, calculating gleam of his eyes. He didn't waste energy on a lost cause, and she knew he no longer looked for her compliance.

The broken medallion flashed in her mind. He'd called it the key to controlling her, then shattered it deliberately. Without it, could he still bend her power to his command?

Every instinct screamed the answer was yes.

"Little hybrid, you will stop where you are."

"Nicu, shut up and focus on Tristan!" Devi countered.

Ember flinched at their arrival, tension coiling in her chest. Were they here to claim her as their prize? To fight over who would control her next?

Ember's fingertips grew numb with cold as she scrambled backward, her movements frantic and uneven. A Fae arrow streaked past, a blur of silver and white that skimmed so close its fletching kissed her lashes.

A warning.

The rope of Tristan's magic lashed against her sapphire

shell. Sparks ignited where the two forces collided, the air between them shimmering with the strain. The protective energy wavered, the Wizard's spell pressing harder, twisting as if testing for the weakest point.

Tristan's grin stretched wide, predatory and gleeful, baring teeth that made her stomach churn. He knew as well as she did how this would end.

Ember clawed at the ground, forcing herself further back, her shield thinning with each inch she gained. Distance. She needed it, even if she wasn't sure it would be enough.

"No!"

Nicu's voice? The Fae's? Or both, tangled in the chaos?

The arrow struck, finding a gap in the shield Tristan had worn down. Agony exploded through her shoulder, radiating outward in waves that ignited every nerve. Her right arm went limp, useless at her side. White light seared her vision. She slipped, her strength lost, the ground tilting beneath her as if the universe itself conspired to send her spiraling.

The pain ebbed, swallowed by the relentless brilliance that consumed her senses. Sound vanished. Thought scattered.

This was how Tristan won.

29

NICU

The forest blurred around Nicu in a rush of shifting greens and browns, the terrain as familiar as the Ink on his skin. The Fae followed on his trail. Altaya's presence weighed the most, their magic hovering at the edge of his senses as if they meant to stay far enough away to avoid getting sucked in by his tattoos. If they knew he could manipulate their power from a distance, perhaps the spell would disappear.

For years he'd run the forests of Trifecta as he crisscrossed the miles and trailed the hybrid girl he was destined to leave behind. The task had kept him from the Fae while protecting them, maintaining order, his eye always on potential chaos with orders to control it.

Yet it was true Chaos he'd been stalking all along.

Nicu forged ahead, each moment taking him closer to a place he wished to avoid.

Ember was not likely to welcome his presence. He wasn't sure he could bear hers.

A heavy pressure settled behind his brows, carrying a sentience that was distinctly not his own. This was unlike the passive Promise and Wish Magic, which simply followed the flow of potential energy like a breeze. An undeniable Force latched onto him, tracking his every move and sifting through each thought with relentless precision.

Nicu steadied his mind, focusing on the rhythm of his body's movements. The path toward choice might be inevitable, but he would make it as winding and prolonged as possible.

"So." Devi's voice carried effortlessly as she matched Nicu's sprint through the forest with a casual stride. It appeared she'd not only deciphered Tristan's spell but also enhanced it, enabling her to remain visible and converse while keeping pace.

A subtle ripple of magic extended from her, weaving into his space. Nicu examined its intricate design before letting it envelop them both. Altaya's displeased grunt reached his ears, a clear sign they'd sensed the shift. However, the spell ensured the Fae would no longer hear whatever Devi meant to discuss.

"You came back from death."

"I had not died just yet."

Devi blinked, startled by the immediate and unfiltered response. She hadn't expected such honesty. Nicu hadn't intended to offer it, but now that the words were out, he resolved to follow wherever the conversation led.

"Of course not. It was a foolish notion. The dead should not be brought back."

Ah. Her thoughts had turned to her mother, then. Still, the privacy spell lingered, suggesting Devi's mind held more than just grief.

"Do you think Ember is in trouble? Or is she the danger?"

The question of the hour. "I am withholding expectations."

Devi snorted, the sound sharp and unrestrained, as if to shake off the lingering shadows of mourning. Her gaze softened, sliding past him, the spark of contemplation flaring in her expression. Was she working through a puzzle, or searching for one to solve? Perhaps she needed a distraction.

"Are you going to save her?"

Nicu weighed the question, the gravity of it pressing against him. An impulsive answer could carry consequences he wasn't ready to face. The brief glimpse of Ember offered no clear sense of her intentions, leaving him with nothing definitive to anchor his response.

"Would you?" he countered, his voice steady, the words measured.

Devi raised a hand to examine her nail beds, her spelled path deftly avoiding obstacles to keep her feet moving smoothly. "I would offer a trade."

"I need nothing."

"I have discovered something," Devi offered. "Connections in the magics. Tattoo. Veil. Trimark."

"Things already owed," he reminded her.

"Yet the information I possess exceeds the value of our original agreement, and it's time to revisit the terms."

Nicu dodged a rocky outcrop as he considered her suggestion. Without Edan, his sources of intelligence were few. Perhaps Devi had something worth tipping the scales.

"What is your price?" he asked once they were in line again.

"A real answer to a question. No faery connotation or twists of tongue. No evasion." They had arrived at the heart of why Devi cast the privacy spell, shielding their conversation from the Fae. Nicu inclined his head in restrained agreement.

"Which side are you on, Nicu Coccia?"

A crushing weight settled on Nicu's shoulders as though the universe itself sought to pin him down. Only the relentless pace of his run kept him upright, momentum forcing his body forward even as his mind threatened to unravel. He pressed his lips together, focusing every ounce of willpower on silencing the fragmented thoughts clawing for dominance. Fae versus Trimarked. Duty versus choice. He refused to let the arguments merge into something he couldn't ignore.

Leave it to Devi to prod the one wound he needed untouched. She didn't want a Fae answer, but that was all he could offer her now.

"You will have to be more precise if you require a specific reply."

"A series of questions, then. Good or evil?"

"Good." The word snapped out, sharp with the frustration of having his morality questioned.

"Even if the corruption is Fae?"

Nicu forced his thoughts to remain disciplined, each response carefully boxed away from the storm of Chaos and Fate hovering over his decisions.

"There has been much evil in our pasts and always vanquished."

"Evasion."

Nicu refused to grind his teeth, particularly when faced with what should be an easy question. He kept his interpretation compartmentalized. The Fae had not proven dishonorable in this. His answer for Devi did not mean he'd made a decision for Chaos.

"Yes."

Devi paused, her eyes sharpened for the strike.

"Ember or Trifecta?"

Nicu's steps faltered. Devi might not have seen the miss. Altaya was sure to have.

How had she hit so close to his agreement with Chaos and Fate? Were the Powers influencing her? Did she see something he did not?

"What would you do?"

Devi lost all impressions of a smile, the drop of her lips highlighting the dark half-moons below her eyes. "You cannot walk this line forever, Nicu. I repeat with emphasis on your intelligence and mine. Which side are you on?"

Nicu's eyes narrowed, piecing together Devi's hidden meaning.

"Logic suggests you claim all Fae are evil."

"Overstatement." Her snarl was sharp enough to bite.

"What are you after? You ask for a simple answer, but your inquiry is unclear."

"I've come to understand you. It was Promise Magic that brought your almost-death. I know which forces can stitch you back together and return you to this realm. It is not from Aaron's ill-spoken wish."

Nicu fell into a thoughtful silence.

"What information do you have to trade?" A gentle way of saying that the secrets he held did not automatically belong to her, no matter how accurate her guesses. Now she must prove that her knowledge was valuable enough for his answer.

"The Fae have tied Ember's magic to something physical."

"Yes."

Devi's eyes flashed with irritation as she realized he was already aware.

"You are connected to Ember with Veil magic."

New intelligence, but not surprising. Nicu was willing to consider a trade, depending on how much more she shared. "How long have you known?"

"I suspected pieces for a while, but it wasn't until I tried to revive you that I understood the true depth of the link between you, Ember, and the Veil."

"What does the Veil connection mean?"

"It's not a strong tie, like your Promise was. I'd guess it's why your magic behaves the way it does. I can't tell you more without additional study." Devi pursed her lips and looked at the sky. "You know what Ember's object is, don't you?"

"Yes."

"And you used it?"

"Which inquiry do you prefer an answer to?" She did not have enough leverage to acquire both.

"The first one in contention," Devi clarified through clenched teeth.

"You assume my return is tied to where my loyalties lie. As if those universal powers would care."

"When it comes to Ember?"

Devi's rhetorical question stood as testament to her brilliance and power. She had seen the fractured pieces and guessed at the picture they formed.

"What will you do, Nicu?"

Her original request, rephrased and incredibly vague. She had traded well, though.

"Not even Fate knows that answer."

Devi's expression darkened, her narrowed eyes and pursed lips hinting at a brewing argument. But the moment stretched, and instead of pressing forward, her flush faded. Her mouth softened, a wry understanding settling over her features.

"Only you could manage to balance on such a thin and dangerous line," she murmured, her tone both resigned and sharp.

Devi allowed her spell to drop, and Nicu immediately sensed Altaya's power creeping closer. He ignored the tension building behind him, focusing instead on the greater challenge looming ahead. No Man's drew near, and his breaths deepened, the effort making conversation impossible. The towering trees thinned, parting to reveal the massive trunk of the forbidden sequoia.

It had grown, its base spreading to dominate most of No Man's. The branches reached skyward, bending outward against the invisible barrier that had trapped them all in Trifecta for two decades. Nicu filed away that revelation, his attention snapping to the tree's new girth. He was concerned it would obstruct his view of Tristan and Ember, assuming they were still there. Adjusting his path, he veered toward the Fae boundary, as he was not given passage onto Witch territory.

Ember Lee scrambled backwards on the ground, inches from the Fae border. Her skin was pale and damp, with flushed cheeks beneath wide, frantic eyes. What was left of her hair hung in ragged, singed strands, exposing the tattoo on the back of her neck—an unmistakable mark that sent a cold wave through Nicu.

"Trimarked. Stop!" The sound of Altaya's bow string tightening stiffened every muscle in Nicu's body. Devi continued forward without hesitation, but Nicu froze, unwilling to risk startling Ember into crossing the boundary.

"Little hybrid." His voice was rough, deliberate, the nickname meant to anchor her, to cut through her fear and trigger her ingrained habit of challenging him. "You will stop where you are."

Devi shouted something about Tristan, but Nicu did not care about the Wizard. He was not tied to Nicu's fate. Altaya's bowstring released, sending a warning arrow zipping past Ember. Nicu clenched his jaw, resisting the urge to chastise Altaya for their heavy-handedness. Finesse would have served better here.

Ember's limbs jerked as she scrambled further back. Her eyes were laser-focused on something ahead of her, her full-body shield flickering faintly. Why wasn't she listening?

Nicu saw the answer too late.

Tristan emerged from behind the massive sequoia, his spell unfurling like a coiled serpent. A thick, pulsing rope of magic stretched toward Ember, crafted to wrap around her and bind more than just her power. Stronger than the Hive Queen's control, this would take away Ember's autonomy. All her will.

Was this what she had been fighting?

Nicu's chest tightened. He had truly failed her.

And yet, Chaos had returned him. A second chance. Though he wasn't ready to choose between the paths laid before him, he could act now, work to repair the present enough to buy them both more time.

"No!" Nicu's voice thundered as he extended his power toward Tristan's magic with the intent of seizing and unraveling the rope before it reached Ember.

"No!" Altaya's shout overlapped his, sharp and commanding. Their bowstring snapped, and the second arrow flew fast and true, cutting through the air with deadly precision.

Ember's cry split the tension as the arrow struck deep into her upper arm. Her shield wavered, momentarily dimmed.

White light engulfed the clearing, a searing brightness that devoured every shadow. A sharp, deafening crack rang out, like the sound of shattering glass magnified a hundredfold. Nicu's knees buckled, and he hit the ground hard, his breath stolen by the unseen force that slammed into his core. The marks of Chaos and Fate etched into his skin blazed like molten fire.

As the light faded, the world seemed unnaturally quiet. The sequoia's uppermost branches swung freely, brushing against the unfiltered sky. Above them, the dome was no longer whole. From a massive rupture at the barrier's summit, thin spiderweb cracks radiated outward, converging into thick fractures that disappeared toward Trifecta's outskirts.

"This. This is not right!" Tristan howled, his voice raw with rage and disbelief.

"Something I'm sure the Coven will be eager to hear you explain," Devi growled, her power sparking like static at the edges of Nicu's consciousness.

Altaya stepped to Nicu's side, their body trembling with restrained energy as they both fixed their gaze on a single point —where No Man's Land kissed the edge of Fae territory. There, defying all logic, a solitary sprout emerged. It was fragile and defiant, half-rooted in death and half in life, a thin green stalk standing against the icy grasp of Trifecta's winter.

But it was not the sign Nicu sought.

His breath caught, chest tightening as his gaze swept the clearing, then beyond into the Fae lands. The reality before him remained unchanged—impossible and unforgiving.

Ember Lee was gone.

30

EMBER

The sound of boots over rock shattered the silence. Wherever Ember landed was unforgiving. Rough, jagged stones pressed into her left shoulder and hip. She shifted, trying to ease the pressure, but stopped as a fiery pulse flared through her right arm.

Ember eased heavy lashes open, only to squeeze them shut against a blinding light. A haze of red-tinted brightness filtered through her eyelids, the air thick with fine, sunlit dust motes that stung her eyes and throat. The rock dug into her ribs, a solid reminder of her body's battered state.

Memories flickered, piecing themselves together in disjointed fragments. Tristan's snarling commands. The towering sequoia. Nicu's voice cutting through the chaos. And then the Fae.

The arrow.

Holy fades. She'd been shot.

Her breath hitched as the distant rhythm of boots striking stone grew louder, deliberate in their approach. Someone was coming.

With a deep inhale, Ember braced her left arm against the ground, leveraging herself upright. A sharp, whimpered cry slipped through her clenched teeth as every muscle in her body rebelled. Her limbs trembled under the effort, but she couldn't stay here. She had to move.

Ember's second attempt at opening her eyes fared better. Prepared for the onslaught, her irises adjusted to the searing brightness. She focused on the arrow first. The shaft was thin, and the arrowhead had passed clean through, though her thick coat sleeve mercifully obscured the actual damage. Unsure what to do about her wound, Ember lifted her attention to her surroundings. She froze as the stark landscape unfolded before her.

This was not Trifecta.

Uneven rocks jutted out from the barren, sun-bleached ground, their edges smoothed and worn by an unrelenting wind. Fine, pale dust swirled in the air. The pink tint of the sky cast an otherworldly glow across the desolate expanse.

Ember's pulse jumped at the sound of soles on stone. The faint scrape of dust drew Ember's attention to the approaching figure. Leather straps crisscrossed calves sculpted with solid muscle. An angled skirt revealed the curve of one powerful thigh while concealing the other, its fabric bunched under a tan leather corset that guarded her ribs and heart, climbing to circle her throat in a thick band.

One bare arm bore spiraling tattoos that twisted like smoke, while the other carried a simpler design. A single spiral began at her collarbone and wound its way to her wrist, ending in a serpent's head inked into the basin of her palm. The snake's shaded eyes glared up at Ember as the stranger crouched beside her, forearms resting on her knees.

This woman was Fae.

A cold realization settled over her. In her desperation to escape Tristan, she must have crossed the Fae boundary. Nicu's shouts, the Fae's warning arrows. Ember's pounding head struggled to hold onto the threads of understanding that refused to make sense when she was clearly not surrounded by redwoods.

Ember closed her eyes, her energy draining out of her. It didn't matter if this Fae was friend or foe. She couldn't tell the difference anymore. Taking a long, trembling inhale, she focused on the rhythm of her heartbeat. Vibrations hummed through her bones, soothing the relentless ache in her shoulder.

Pain, sudden and searing, tore a scream from her throat. Ember's eyes flew open, tears blurring her vision as she gasped for air. The Fae crouched before her, holding the arrow's shaft in two cleanly severed pieces, one in each hand. Somehow the woman had sliced through the wood and pulled the arrow free without Ember noticing until it was done.

Green-glass eyes flitted over Ember, head to toe and back again. The Fae tucked the broken projectile into her belt, then reached behind her waist to claim a strip of cloth from some hidden pocket.

Ember's muscles tensed as the Fae leaned closer, the air between them heavy with the scent of sunbaked earth and something metallic. Whatever this was—help, indifference, or some twisted sense of amusement—Ember couldn't tell, and the ambiguity set her nerves on edge.

"What are you doing?" Ember asked, her voice thin and strained. The Fae didn't answer, instead lifting Ember's arm just enough to wrap it over the blood-soaked coat. Ember's head dipped as her vision darkened, the sharp pain threatening to drag her into unconsciousness.

Whether it was magic woven into the cloth or a silent spell cast with deft subtlety, relief swept through her. A gentle chill crept into the searing heat of her shoulder, easing the tension knotting her muscles until her entire arm felt blissfully numb.

"Thank you." Ember's voice wavered, hopeful the danger had passed. "Where am I?"

The woman's arched brow rose. "Gypsum."

Ember straightened, a sharp jolt of pain reminded her hasty movements weren't in her best interest. She clutched her right elbow and looked around the pale desert landscape once more. This was Gypsum? The Fae realm?

"How in the verge did I get here?"

"I am not sure. I came to investigate a disturbance and found you. You must have come through the Veil. Terran, I assume? How did you pass through? It has been locked for hundreds of years."

"Wait, what? How do I go back?" she blurted, panic rising in her chest. Even Terra might be safer than a realm filled with Fae. Safer being a relative term.

"Not a clue." The Fae's response was as sharp as it was final. "Unless you can traverse the Veil again."

Ember took a deep breath and searched out with her senses. There was no Veil energy to find. No dome. No Fae or Witch boundaries marked with vines and magic.

"It doesn't look like it," she whispered

The woman's casual shrug did nothing to soothe Ember. "Appears as if you are stuck, then."

She stood in one powerful movement, readjusting the confiscated arrows at her belt. Ember's chest tightened, panicked at the prospect of being abandoned in a place marked by nothingness. Instinct more than logic drove her magic to stir, flickering weakly from her depleted reserves. It pulled what little energy remained, forming a faint, almost invisible shield over her skin.

The Fae froze mid-step, her sharp eyes narrowing. Had she noticed the flicker? Or sensed the hum of power?

"Who are you?"

Ember licked her dry lips, relieved the Fae hadn't left, but still wary of trusting her.

"What are you asking?"

The scowl disappeared behind a brilliantly white smile.

"Now that was almost Fae. Fine. Names first. Mine is Shade."

Okay. "Ember."

"Are you human?"

"Are you Fae?" Ember countered, hoping that deflecting with the obvious might lead Shade to assume the same about her answer.

Shade leaned back onto her heels, her posture relaxing as her eyes softened with amusement and perhaps a little respect.

"You are from that city in Terra where humans and mages are trapped, correct?"

Ember pinched her lips together, trying to keep her breath steady. "How do you know about that?"

"The living cannot pass between realms, but objects can. I have raised a fine profit trading with those stuck on Terra, and have learned a few things."

Shade crouched and gripped Ember's ribs with firm hands, taking over most of the effort to get her upright. Once Ember was on her feet, Shade eased away, keeping close in case Ember's wobble turned into something more significant.

"So, little copula, how have you, as a human, become touched by a god?"

"What?" The words echoed in Ember's head, resonating against a memory she struggled to bring forward. Something about Goddess touched? No. Born.

"Our eyes," Shade continued. "Most Fae irises are so dark, you can't tell what color they are. Ours, however, have been washed out by contact with the supposed divine. If you are unaware, then your encounter has not come yet. How nice that must be."

Shade's lips twisted, her expression betraying the sour taste of her own words. Ember fought the urge to sink back to the ground, the enormity of somehow being involved with a god threatening to overtake her. Shade could be wrong. Transparent eye colors might be more common on Terra.

Nicu's eyes were pale, too.

Ember shoved the thought aside, unwilling to linger on him.

"Now, tell me." Shade drew out her pause. "Why do you wear Binding Ink?"

The hand of Ember's good arm flew up to her neck. Her hair had burned away in Trifecta, though her skin was intact, exposing her Trimarked Tattoo.

Ember grit her teeth, then settled on a partial answer to two of Shade's questions. "Half human."

Shade's gaze swept over Ember once more, deliberate and unhurried, starting at her feet and climbing back up to meet her eyes.

"Not half Fae."

"Witch."

"But Fae Ink. For what reason?"

"What else?" Ember demanded. "Control."

It wasn't a lie. Shade's pursed lips indicated she'd wanted a different answer.

The Fae woman's eyes flicked toward the sky, or so Ember assumed until a peculiar, high-pitched thunder rolled through the air.

"What was that?" A shiver wracked Ember's exhausted muscles, her shoulder twinging through the numbing spell.

"A dragon." Shade responded as if it were nothing, but the tooth-baring smile suggested otherwise. "We Fae have a truce with them. It does not extend to humans. Or Witches," she added, covering all of Ember's blood.

What about a half mage born on Fae soil?

Ember kept that question to herself, well-schooled in the power and protection of secrets.

"It would be wise for you to stay with me." Her statement lacked the warmth of a heartfelt welcome.

"What's the catch?"

Shade righted her posture and gave a firm nod. "Smart to

ask. I will tell you later. For now, you can choose between me, or them."

The shadow swooped closer, its serrated wings slicing the air with a grace that belied its size. Ember's breath snagged in her throat, her heart pounding a chaotic rhythm against her ribs. She snapped her gaze to Shade, only to find the Fae walking away, her tone maddeningly calm as she threw a parting remark over her shoulder.

"Better decide quick."

31

EPILOGUE
BRANNA

*B*ranna Kaplan shivered against the pine needle cushion where she'd collapsed, her shadows so consuming that the forest beyond was a vague, muffled nothing.

She'd walked away from Nicu; had been happy to. The moment he fell, a strange awakening had unfurled within her. The edges of the world shimmered with pearlescent light, revealing new details. Edan's form had become startlingly clear to her eyes, his presence no longer a mere suggestion but almost solid, as if the veil of death between them had thinned.

Nicu's loss had proven her freedom. It shattered the anchor holding her back. For the first time, she could explore the power humming through her veins, unfettered.

Her exaltation had been short-lived. A seismic wave of energy tore through her, striking at the base of her spine and igniting every nerve ending with white-hot agony. She crawled across the forest floor, collapsing against the base of a redwood. Shadows coiled tightly around her, shielding her vulnerability from the world.

Weeks ago, Nicu barely touched the latch on the Trimarked medallion, and even that had brought her to her knees. Tonight, the pain returned tenfold as the world fractured around her. First Branna's. Then Trifecta's.

If she hadn't been suffering so much, she might have laughed at the irony.

Nicu must have activated his fading talisman. It was the only explanation that fit. She'd always known he would choose Ember over her. It wasn't a surprise. Only Edan had ever chosen Branna. But as a ghost, he was a mere echo of who he used to be.

The pale lines on Branna's skin expanded beneath her tattoos, no longer confined by the sweeping curves of Ink shaped like Death's scythe. She studied the spreading color with a detached curiosity. At first, she'd thought the discoloration was gray, but now it emerged as an otherworldly matte silver—like steel that refused to shine. In sunlight, it might gleam, but here in the shadows, it carried an eerie weight, as if her death as an infant was finally catching up to her.

Wouldn't Nicu love that.

Except, as time passed, the tension gave way to an unfamiliar calm. The silvery lines continued to spread across her dark skin, but instead of draining her, they seemed to feed her. Energy seeped into her limbs, quiet but undeniable.

Ghostly whispers tickled her ears, growing louder until they were unmistakable. Branna lifted her head, her heart beating faster.

She'd always needed intense focus to hear spirits before. Now their voices overlapped, a cacophony of stories and secrets, like Halfers crowded into one of their cramped houses, murmuring tales to each other.

With a steadying breath, Branna dropped her shadows.

Trifectan ghosts gathered close, their presence familiar yet strange in this new clarity. They weren't transparent beings, but faded, their tones muted and textures blurred. The longer they'd been dead, the more frayed their edges became, like old blankets loved for too long.

One spirit stepped forward, parting the sea of spectral forms with an ease that spoke of authority. His lines were sharp, his presence vivid—a testament to how recently he'd crossed into this life without a body. Even the jagged spikes of his tattoos stood out, dark and defined.

"Edan."

"Branna, you are Falling." His voice cracked and his index finger traced the back of her hand. The shock of his touch paled in comparison to the icy chill his words drove into her veins.

"What?"

"Your skin. It is happening faster than I have ever seen." Edan's eyes met hers with fierce determination.

"Fae are not meant to live in this realm, Branna. Those outside Trifecta have already Fallen. With the barrier cracked open, more of our people will Fall."

Branna's spine stiffened. The Fae were not her people.

Edan caught her reaction, his frown deepening. "The Fallen do nothing but destroy."

Her voice lashed out before she could stop herself. "What exactly do you think I can do about it?"

Edan's eyes softened, and this time his touch felt heavy with apology. "We need the Trimarked Girl to fix this. The barrier must be repaired."

Branna's chest tightened as his next words fell, low and final. "The Fallen are on their way. If they breach the barrier, they will not stop until they have consumed every soul in Trifecta."

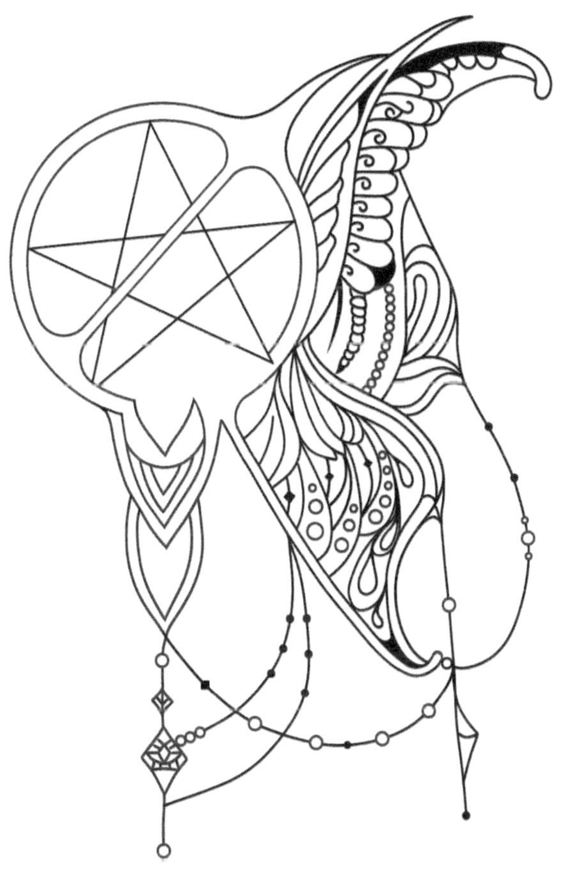

ACKNOWLEDGMENTS

This book fought me every step of the way. It challenged me, broke me down, and demanded more than I ever thought I could give. Yet, here it is, finished and ready to be shared—all because of the incredible support system I've been blessed to have.

To my family, who made space for me to write even when life didn't. For understanding when my mind was lost in Trifecta's struggles, even when we were supposed to be on vacation. Your patience and love kept me grounded.

To my Quill & Cup family, who believed in this story when I struggled to. Your encouragement, insight, and unwavering support were the light I needed to find my way through every dark draft. This book exists because you stood with me.

And to every reader who finds themselves in Ember's fight, who feels the weight of impossible choices—this story is for you. May you find the strength to defy the paths laid before you and carve your own way.

Thank you, all of you, for being part of this journey.

ABOUT THE AUTHOR

C.K. Sorens, a USA Today Bestselling author of Defiant Fantasy, writes dark fantasy and romantasy that explore fate, choice, and resilience. Known for her character-driven stories and compelling worlds, Sorens' works include the urban fantasy Trimarked series and the romantasy *Eighteen Wishes*. When not writing, she enjoys hiking, puzzles, and family adventures.

Discover more about C.K. Sorens' worlds of Defiant Fantasy and explore her latest releases at www.cksorens.com.

instagram.com/ck_sorens
bookbub.com/profile/c-k-sorens